D1302009

TWICE REMOVED

An FBI Thriller (Book 2)

DOUGLAS DOROW

 **MTSPress**

ISBN-13 978-0-9994862-1-4

For my family and for my father-in-law for raising a wonderful daughter and for introducing me to the wonders of Otter Tail County and South Lake Lida where this story is set.

CHAPTER ONE

"All aboard!" The conductor stood outside the Amtrak train and swung her flashlight over her head. Passengers milled about outside the train, enjoying the pleasant summer evening before they boarded. The lights on the platform winked on as the late summer light faded into dark.

The Union Depot stood on the edge of downtown St. Paul. It used to serve people who traveled north on the Mississippi via paddle wheel steamboats, who then transferred to the train to travel into the plains of the Midwest.

The refurbished depot was now a transportation hub for Amtrak, hauling people between Chicago and the West Coast and for busses taking people to one of the casinos in Minnesota, Wisconsin, or the Megabus to Chicago.

"All abooooooooard!" the conductor sang again with a bluesy flourish. People on the platform clapped as she brought her boarding call to its end. Passengers started to make their way to the entrances of the different train cars.

"She's got a nice voice, doesn't she?" FBI Special Agent

Jack Miller stood with a team crowded into the baggage room of the Amtrak Station, approximately thirty yards back from the tracks at the west end of the platform. "A frustrated singer, I bet."

The baggage room lights were off. The agents stood back from the door in the shadows, waiting for the operation to begin. Behind Jack, stood Special Agent Mary Kiley, officer Jones, a representative of Amtrak security, and DEA Supervisory agent Del Toro, from the Chicago office. Kiley said, "She won't be singing when we delay their departure."

Jack glanced at his watch: Ten-oh-five. Five minutes to the scheduled departure of the westbound Empire Builder continuing on its trek from Chicago to Seattle. The operation was going to start right at departure time to make sure all passengers had arrived. The engineers would be made aware of the delay in a couple of minutes.

Two plain, gray-colored delivery trucks rolled up to each end of the train and Jack ticked through the plan in his head. Inside the trucks were FBI and DEA agents in protective vests with their agency initials on them. Amtrak security, posing as maintenance workers, were positioned in the station cleaning window. Their cleaning buckets and Slippery When Wet signs in place to keep people from looking out the windows so they couldn't see what was going on and potentially warn people on the train.

A DEA agent standing behind Del Toro held a German Shepherd on a short leash as it pulled, ready to go to work.

"Who knows we're coming?" Jack asked.

"Just the engineers," the Amtrak security officer answered. "I just let them know they're not going anywhere for a while."

"Do you sing?" Jack asked Kiley.

"Badly, in my car or in the shower."

Jack's cell phone buzzed. He grabbed a quick look at the text and slipped the phone back into his pocket.

"Softball game over?" Kiley asked.

Jack nodded. "We won."

"Sorry you had to miss it for this. Catch the next one?"

"Last game of summer," Jack said.

"That sucks."

"Yep." Jack thought about the disappointment on his daughter's face when Julie again told her, Dad wasn't going to be able to make it to her game. It wasn't the first promise to her he broke, and not the last. He rubbed the cell phone in his pocket and keyed his radio with his other hand. "Status check."

Each of the teams replied back with their readiness.

Jack's hands tingled and his focus sharpened as adrenalin pumped into his system. He saw the tension in agent Del Toro, flexing and shaking his hands to get them stilled. The dog started to whine, sensing the start of the operation. "Ready to go?" Jack asked over his shoulder.

Del Toro replied with a thumbs-up signal and the Amtrak agent answered with a short, "Ready." Jack took a deep breath, blew it out and keyed his radio again. "Operation Westward Ho begins in three, two, one. Go, go, go."

On the first Go, the teams in the trucks at either end of the train moved into action. The back doors of the trucks rolled up and agents deployed to their assignments. The first agents out corralled anybody still standing on the platform. The next group of agents deployed on either side of the train to guard the doors. The last group of agents entered each of the cars to secure the car and tell people to stay calm.

Jack and his crew strode out onto the platform to observe the operation. An FBI agent entered the Amtrak car closest to the rear, followed by the DEA agent with the dog. All of the checked luggage had been inspected by the dog and an agent before it was loaded on the train. They hadn't found anything.

The FBI agent would walk through the train assuring the passengers that they were just doing a quick check before the train left and observe the passengers for telltale signs of hiding something as well as provide eyes for the DEA agent who would be focused on leading the dog to check them and their carry-on luggage.

"The intel is solid?" Jack asked Del Toro.

"The big boys are moving harder drugs into the Dakota oil patch and it's coming from Chicago or Minneapolis. Fentanyl is getting into the pipeline and that stuff is nasty. This train was supposed to be the one. After this operation, the word will get out we were here and it might move product back onto the highways.

"Well, maybe we'll get a lead if nothing else." Jack waved his hand at the bugs buzzing around his ears. "Damn, I hate these mosquitos. I have to keep moving around so they don't eat me alive." He walked away from the group and paced along the platform, monitoring the progress of the agents in the train through the car windows and with radio checks.

Voices boomed in Jack's earpiece. Somebody on the train was making a run for it. A man burst out of the center Amtrak car door. The agent stationed there knocked him to the ground, trained his gun at his back, and screamed at him. "Don't move!"

Jack ran to assist. He kneeled on the man's back, put a hand on the back of his head, and leaned over so the man would hear him. "Put your arms out to the side."

The young man grunted, "What did I do?"

"Put your hands out to your sides," Jack said. The man complied. Jack grabbed a hand and twisted it behind the man's back. Agent Kiley joined Jack and put a zip tie around his left wrist. She looped another tie through that one and then secured that to the right wrist that Jack had pulled back.

"What'd I do?" the man mumbled with his cheek still pushed into the pavement.

"You ran," Jack said. "And Agent Kiley here is going to talk to you about where you were off to in such a hurry." Jack and Kiley rolled the man onto his back and then helped him sit up. "You got him?" Jack asked Kiley. She nodded, helped him to his feet, and directed the man to the garage they were working from.

Jack continued to walk the platform, monitoring the operation. The radio chatter told him they hadn't really found anything except a couple of small stashes for personal use or to sell to make a little money. The intel looked like it didn't hold up. "Del Toro, where are you?" Jack asked into the radio.

In his earpiece, Jack heard the reply. "We're wrapping things up."

"Kiley, that guy have anything?" Jack waited for a reply.

"Just some pills that weren't his in his pocket. He was scared."

A glance at his watch told Jack that they'd been going about ten minutes. A quick op. They were almost done. They'd be ready to release the train soon. He surveyed the platform and the activity around him.

A young man hustling across the train platform from the far end caught Jack's attention. He wore a baseball hat, jeans, black boots, and a black t-shirt. He was looking at his phone and carrying a backpack. His head popped up. He appeared to look at the commotion around the train and stopped. Jack couldn't see his eyes, but he knew he was looking at them. Jack smiled, to alleviate any fears, not sure if the guy could see his face or not. He raised his left hand in a signal of Hi or Wait. The guy spun and sprinted in the opposite direction.

"Stop! FBI!" Jack took off after the runner. He yelled into his radio, "I've got another runner. Heading west towards Sibley."

The guy sprinted past the busses loading passengers to go to the casinos. People scattered out of his way.

Jack ran as fast as he could to keep the guy in sight. In his ear, he heard Kiley ask, "You want any help? How about the dog?"

"Finish searching the train. I'll get him," Jack answered. "Stop! ... FBI!" he yelled at the runner. Not quite as loud as before, gasping between the words. The weight of the gear: the vest, extra rounds of ammo, gun, cuffs, flashlight, and phone bounced as he ran. He brushed the ball cap off his head in a useless move to help him speed up.

The runner crossed Kellogg Boulevard and turned right around the corner of a parking garage.

Jack slowed as he approached the corner. He drew his Glock from its holster. "Kiley, I'm pursuing him north, up Sibley."

At the corner of the building, Jack stopped and chanced a quick peek. The guy ran up the street, still carrying his backpack. Jack thought there had to be something in the bag. He would've dropped it if it wasn't valuable. He holstered his weapon and ran after him.

It was slightly uphill, making the run harder. A block ahead at the cross street, a light rail train that carried commuters between the downtowns of St. Paul and Minneapolis sat in the station. Jack pushed harder to catch the runner before he boarded the train.

The chime of the train signaled it was getting ready to leave the station. An older couple walked hand-in-hand down the sidewalk towards them. "Stop, FBI!" Jack yelled. The young man started to run around them. The older man reached for him and got dragged down. The runner bounced off a parked car, fell to the ground. He looked back at Jack and scrambled to his feet.

Jack closed the distance and pushed hard to catch him.

The light rail train started to move, its bell chiming. The guy ran for the front car.

He missed it, Jack thought. The guy veered left like he was racing the train. Jack followed. He was close, debating to dive for the guy or grab the bag. He reached out and grabbed a strap on the backpack. The guy stumbled, twisted and got one arm out of the backpack, then the other. He spun around, keeping his footing and ran in front of the moving train and crossed the tracks. The engineer blew the horn as the train continued forward.

Jack couldn't follow. The train had moved too far along for him to run in front of it and still catch the guy. He tried to watch the guy through the windows of the train cars as they passed, but the lights from inside the cars reflected off the glass, making it hard for him to see out the other side. He ran back to the approaching end car. It passed and Jack ran across the tracks and up the street to where he'd last seen the guy.

He was gone.

Jack put out a call for the St. Paul police with a description and last known location, but didn't think they'd find him.

Jack put an arm through a strap of the backpack and threw it over his shoulder. He retraced his steps back to the station. He stopped to make sure the couple that had tried to help was OK. Then he returned to the platform to join the group of agents. Sweat dripped down his forehead and the sides of his head.

"Lost him, huh?" Kiley asked. She handed Jack his FBI ball cap.

"Got his backpack, but not him." Jack set the pack down and wiped the sweat from his face. "How about here?"

"The dog got a couple more hits on passengers' carry-on baggage. We're detaining their owners." Kiley answered.

"Let's back away from the bag and bring the dog over to check it out. We don't know what's in there or why he ran," Jack said.

The group formed a circle around the bag, standing back about twenty feet.

"What happened? How did he lose you?" Kiley asked.

"I almost had him. Got a hold of the bag. He twisted and got his arms out of it just in time to run in front of the light rail as it left the station. I got stuck on this side."

The handler arrived and gave the dog a command and it ran to the bag and sniffed it. It started whining. The handler grabbed the dog by the collar and attached the lead to control him.

"He's signaling drugs present," the handler said.

"No explosives?" Jack asked.

"Now you think of that?" Kiley asked.

Jack shrugged. "I just picked it up. Pretty sure it was drugs, but thought I'd ask."

"He's trained for both," the handler answered. "If there were explosives, he'd signal different. He'd just sit. There are drugs in the bag."

Jack squatted and slowly zipped open the backpack. He shined his flashlight in it to make sure there weren't any surprises. Then he started dumping the contents out on the ground. "Quite the stash in here: a regular pharmacy of prescription and packaged drugs. No wonder he didn't want to give it up."

Agent Del Toro picked up a couple of plastic-wrapped bundles. He wore latex gloves. "I'd guess these are heroin and fentanyl. At least these drugs aren't making it to the oil patch, or wherever they were going. We put a pretty big dent in somebody's supply."

The conductor walked over to the group of agents. "Gentlemen, ma'am, can we leave? I have a schedule to keep. You've already made me late."

Jack stood. "You've got a nice voice. Sing anywhere besides train platforms?"

"You can find me at The Jazz Club in Chicago, sweetheart. Now can we go?"

"All aboard," Jack said.

THE AGENTS GATHERED BACK in the Amtrak baggage room. "Not a total bust, I guess. We'll wrap things up in the situation room at HQ in the morning," Jack said.

"We got it, Jack," Kiley replied. "You're on vacation, as of now. Two weeks, right?"

"Two weeks?" Del Toro said. "Maybe I should switch to the FBI."

Jack chuckled. "Who has time to take vacation?"

"You do," Kiley said. "The boss's orders. Really. He said you're done tonight." She gestured at Del Toro. "We've got this."

"I wouldn't fight two weeks of vacation," Del Toro said. "How do you get two weeks of vacation?"

Kiley stepped in front of Jack and stared into his eyes. "Solve a big case, save the world and you get two weeks at a cabin on one of Minnesota's ten thousand lakes." She put a hand on his chest and gave him a little push. "Now, go take your family on vacation, catch some fish and use sunscreen. We got this."

"Yes, ma'am," Jack said.

CHAPTER TWO

The house was dark. Jack let himself into the kitchen from the garage and turned on the lights over the island. Vince met him at the door, his nails clacking on the floor, his tail wagging. "Hey, buddy. Everybody else sleeping?" Jack pet him on the head and then Vince turned and left to find his own place to sleep.

"Jack?"

"I'm home." Jack wandered into the family room and found Julie on the couch in the dark. He sat down on the end, put her feet in his lap and started massaging one of them. He pressed his thumb into her arch and found a tight spot.

"Mmm," she purred. "That feels good. How'd it go tonight?"

"It went fine. Nobody got hurt. Wasn't an A-plus op, but I'd give it a B. We got some drugs off the street." Jack thought about the guy that got away and leaving Agent Kiley to finish up the case with Del Toro. Jack didn't like not finishing a case.

Julie mumbled a response.

"Why don't you just wait for me in bed?" Jack asked.

"I wouldn't wake up and know you're OK if I was in bed," Julie responded. "And you wouldn't rub my feet."

Jack put his head back and felt some of his tension release. "A good game tonight?"

"Girls played well. Could've gone either way."

"Sorry I missed it."

"Lynn can tell you all about it tomorrow."

Jack started massaging the other foot. "Ready for vacation?"

"Um-hmm" Julie gently nodded her head. "We're all packed. The kids helped load the car. We just need to get up, grab some breakfast, and coffee and hit the road."

"Thanks for doing that," Jack replied. "A couple of the others on the op tonight were jealous. Two weeks of vacation." Jack was ready for it. The past two months had been good, getting the family back together after a short separation, but he'd still been busy with work, missed games. Two weeks with just the four of them, or the five of them, counting Vince, was going to be good. They could all just have fun, reconnect, show the kids that they were back together as a family before the kids went back to school after Labor Day.

"Did you see the note on the island?" Julie asked.

"Nope. From who?"

"The headhunter. Linda."

Jack stopped rubbing Julie's foot. "I said I'd start with her after vacation."

"She said things are hot now. People know who you are after saving the Fed last month. One of the reasons I came back was because you said you'd find something else to do. Here in Minneapolis with one of the big companies."

"She can't wait two weeks?"

Julie squirmed into a sitting position facing Jack, legs

crossed. "Linda needs to talk to you now to get things lined up while they're hot."

Jack was dreading the conversation. Dreading talking about leaving the FBI and heading up security for one of the Fortune 500 or other big companies in the Twin Cities. It was a promise he made to Julie when she came back home with the kids in July. Missing tonight's game and the others the past couple of weeks didn't help.

He stood up and kissed Julie on the top of her head. "You should go to bed. I'm going to take a shower."

"You'll call her?" Julie asked.

"I'll talk to her this week."

"Call her. Tomorrow," Julie added.

AFTER THE SHOWER, Jack slipped into bed. He heard Julie's steady breathing. She could fall asleep fast when she knew he was home and safe. He didn't know what he was going to say to Linda. Was he really ready to leave the FBI?

He stared at the ceiling and thought about the vacation. Two weeks at the lake. The kids would love it. It had been a long time since he'd gone fishing.

Jack took a couple of deep breaths and concentrated on his own breathing, matching it to Julie's. In and out. In and out. His last thought before he fell asleep was, what was he going to do for two weeks?

CHAPTER THREE

J ack pulled off the gravel road onto the lawn.

"Is this it?" Lynn asked. Both kids leaned over the seats to look through the windshield. Lynn was eight and Willy was six. Vince joined them and wedged his nose between the seats, panting with excitement.

A red cabin with white trim stood surrounded by shade trees. A screened porch on the end faced the lake. "This is it," Jack answered.

"Our lake paradise for two weeks," Julie said. "It looks nice."

The kids bailed out of the car and Vince followed. "We're going to go check out the lake," Lynn yelled.

"Make it quick and then come back and help carry things from the car to the cabin," Julie yelled after them. "Be careful!"

"How long until they're wet?" Jack asked.

Julie laughed. "I think they already are."

Jack leaned over and removed Julie's sunglasses. "Happy vacation," he said. Then he kissed her on the lips. It felt good. No work pressures, a lake adventure with plenty of time to relax.

"Happy vacation," she answered. "This is going to be fun." She put her hands on his chest and gently pushed away. "We need to get this car unloaded."

They pulled a cooler and a couple of suitcases out of the car and hauled them to the cabin.

Jack held the door open for Julie. The screen door slammed shut behind them. Julie jumped. "The sound of summer," Jack said. "I'm sure we'll hear that plenty of times over the next couple of weeks."

Julie stepped into the cabin. "This is nice."

The inside of the cabin reflected the lake life. They stood in a great room: a combination living room and kitchen with double sliding doors that led out to a giant screen porch facing the lake. The walls of the cabin were pine boards. Hanging on the walls were fishing pictures, a collage of old fishing lures, antique cross-country skis. The furniture was made of saplings formed into chairs and a couch covered with cushions.

"Whose is this?" Julie asked.

"A supporter of the FBI makes it available periodically to the SAC. He offered it to us."

Julie took Jack by the hand to explore the cabin. The hallway off the kitchen led back to a couple of bedrooms. Across the living room, a set of stairs led up to a huge loft area. They went up to explore. There were a couple of day beds, a foosball table, and chairs set at tables for games. "The kids are going to like this," Julie said.

"I guess they can stay up here or share the second bedroom downstairs," Jack said.

Julie smiled. "They'll pick up here."

Back on the main floor, Jack sat at the dining table and opened a binder with information on using the cabin;

instructions for turning on the water, the water heater, garbage pick up and use of the speedboat were all detailed. Following pages described things to do in the area, a calendar of events, and some tips on things to consider, like getting a fishing license and bait in Pelican Rapids, the closest town.

The screen door slammed shut, announcing the kids and dog had entered the cabin. They joined Jack at the table. Vince shook himself, off sending a spray of water up around him.

"Wait!" Jack put his arms up to protect himself from getting wet. "I guess you found the lake. How was the water?"

"The lake is great," Willy said.

"What are you doing?" Lynn asked.

"Can we use the boat?"

"I want to go swimming!"

"When can we go fishing?"

"Is there WI-FI?"

Julie walked into the room. "Hold on. We can get started once the car's unloaded. You guys have beds in the loft upstairs. Dad and I have the room back here. How come Vince is wet?"

"We couldn't keep him out of the lake," Lynn said.

"He's a good swimmer," Willy added.

The kids ran up the stairs and Vince followed them up as they all explored the new surroundings.

Jack laughed and pulled Julie onto his lap. "Two weeks. Just us."

"Think they'll slow down?"

"Once the newness is gone, we'll get into our vacation rhythm. Let's get them settled in." Jack kissed Julie's neck and gave her a nudge to get off his lap.

Jack carried their suitcases into their bedroom. Julie followed. They started to unload their bags.

"Give it up, mister." Julie held the gun safe out, the top

flipped open. The safe was the size of a shoebox and had a combination lock.

"I'll feel naked," Jack said.

"Come on. You're on vacation on a small lake. We're swimming, fishing, tanning, barbecuing. You don't need a gun."

"What about the bears?"

Julie held the safe, waiting. "There aren't any bears. And if there are, Vince will chase them away."

Jack stared at Julie. He always carried a gun, and she knew it. This issue had come up before, but he'd never given it up. Julie didn't blink, didn't waver. She stood in front of him, holding the safe. He pulled the holster out from the small of his back and placed the holstered Glock in the safe.

"And your little buddy."

Jack pulled up the leg of his pants, removed the pistol strapped around his ankle and added it to the safe as well. "Happy?" he asked.

"Now you can wear some shorts and get some color on those legs. Cell phone?"

"Leave me something," Jack pleaded.

Julie closed the safe and secured it by spinning the numbers. Then she placed the safe on the top shelf of the closet. "I didn't take your FBI credentials and you can keep the phone for emergencies. No work calls. But I expect you to talk to Linda about the Security Director job. Today. You promised."

"How about after vacation?"

Julie glared at him. "Jack, we talked about this last night. We're doing nothing for the next two weeks. You can find out more about the job and see if it's something worth setting up an appointment to talk with her after vacation."

"Maybe I should just give you my phone." Jack felt the weight of it in his pocket. The headhunter calls started after he solved the big case after the Fourth of July. Linda had won over Julie and was the one he was working with.

Jack wasn't sure if he was an FBI lifer or not. He wasn't in a hurry to get out. But he'd promised Julie he'd look at other opportunities.

"Keep your phone. Now take off your pants."

"What? The kids are just upstairs," Jack said.

Julie smiled and held out a t-shirt, a swimsuit, and a pair of flip-flops. "I don't know what you're thinking. Well, I do. But that will have to wait." She tossed his clothes to him. "Put these on. You're officially on vacation, Mr. Miller. We're going to finish unpacking and go swimming."

JACK, Julie, and the kids sat at the table on the porch and applied sunscreen to their bare skin. Jack stood behind Lynn and spread some over her shoulders and back. "Sorry I had to miss your game last night," he said. "It sounded like it was a great game. A great finish to the season."

"It's OK, Dad. I know you can't make it to all my games because of your job."

"But I would've loved to have been there to watch you play. Mom was sending me text updates, but it's not as good as being there." He finished rubbing the lotion into her skin. "You guys have me for two whole weeks. No job to interrupt us. We'll spend time on the lake, go fishing, see what's in town and the area for us to do."

"Sounds good, Dad," Lynn said.

"I've read the instructions in the binder, so I think I can figure out how to get the boat going. And the swimming beach at the state park is right over there." Jack pointed across the lake to the right of an island. A band of sand was visible between the lake and the green trees. "We'll go get some sun and swim and then we'll head into town for some lunch, groceries and fishing licenses."

The kids grabbed their towels and ran out the door. The screen door slammed shut.

Vince whined at the door, watching them run down the hill.

"You stay here on the porch, buddy, and watch the place. We'll be right back." Jack said.

He grabbed Julie in a hug and kissed her on the lips. "I could get used to this."

"The smell of sunscreen? The slamming screen door?" Julie asked.

"No, kissing you and relaxing family time."

"Talk to the headhunter," she said.

THE SWIMMING BEACH WAS BUSY. People were cooling off in the water, playing in the sand, or sitting at picnic tables, eating and playing games. Jack staked out a spot on the grass and put his towel and bag in a pile. "I'll stay here with our stuff while you guys swim. I'm going to work on my tan."

Julie smiled and shook her head. "Start slow, Jack. You don't want to ruin vacation on the first day with a sunburn."

"Those are some white legs, Dad," Lynn said.

Willy dug a pair of swimming goggles out of their bag.

The sun was high in the sky. The warmth baked Jack as he lay on his beach towel. The noise of the people at the beach and the passing jet skis buzzed as background noise. He relived last night in his mind: the conductor singing, chasing the guy towards the light rail. He wondered if St. Paul PD caught him or how the case discussion went this morning. He thought about calling Agent Kiley and getting an update from her.

Two weeks of this: sun, fishing with the kids, campfires.

He wondered how many days it would take to wind down and then how bad he'd want to wind back up. He opened his eyes and glanced out at Julie and the kids floating and swimming in the lake. He should go join them.

Maybe a quick call to Kiley first. He reached into the bag and felt for his phone. The screen said he'd missed a call from Linda,the headhunter. No loss. He checked again that Julie and the kids were in the lake. Then he started looking for Kiley's number in his phone's address book.

"Jack, help me!" Julie yelled. Jack dropped the phone in the bag. "Damn it, Jack, help me!"

Jack jumped up, ran down to the lake and strode into the water to make his way out to Julie and the kids. The three were standing out about twenty feet from shore. Everyone was safe.

"What's wrong?"

Julie looked at Jack and then down into the lake. "I was standing here fiddling with my ring with my thumb," she showed him repeating the action with her hand. "And it flipped off my finger. It landed in the water right here." Julie pointed down in front of her. "You know, I've lost some weight, my fingers are wet and slippery from the suntan lotion. I'm sorry, Jack."

"That's it? You're OK. The kids are OK? You lost your ring?" Jack reached down to gather some water in his cupped hands, poured it over his head to cool off. "The way you yelled I thought somebody drowned."

"That's it?" Julie asked. The pained look on her face told Jack he'd messed up. "That's a big deal." She stared down into the water. "Don't stir up the sand. Maybe you'll be able to see it."

"Don't worry. We'll find it," Jack said. The water was up past his knees, almost to his crotch. He looked down into the water, trying to focus on the bottom of the lake. The number of swimmers in the area and the slight wind had all sorts of sand and silt floating around and the water sparkled from the sun. "I can kind of see the bottom," he said. "I don't see anything shiny like a ring."

Jack scanned the bottom around them. "Willy, you have goggles. Float around here and see if you can see anything shiny on the bottom."

Willy pulled the goggles down over his eyes and floated in front of Julie. He paddled and lightly kicked, moving around where Julie stood. He stood up. "I don't see anything, Mom."

"Can you look again?" Julie asked. "A little more over there." She pointed out in front of her.

Willy floated some more in the direction Julie pointed. He stood up again. "I can't see much down there. Lots of stuff floating around."

Julie looked disappointed.

"It was only a band," Jack said, trying to make Julie feel better.

"Only a band?" She slapped him on the chest. "Damn it, Jack. After what we went through this year, it's not just a band."

Jack pulled Julie to his chest and hugged her. "I'm sorry," he whispered into her ear. This wasn't a good way to start their vacation. "Stay right there and I'll mark the spot from shore so we can come back later when there aren't so many swimmers here." Jack walked back through the water to the shore. Then he gingerly walked across the sand and rocks in his bare feet to the grass. He turned around and lined up Julie with a cabin across the lake. He looked down and laid some rocks up in a row so he could find the spot again. He carefully picked his steps down to the shore, saving the tender bottoms of his feet and strode purposefully through the water to Julie, counting his steps as he went. When he got to Julie, he wrapped his arms around her. "It's OK. We'll find it."

"You think so?" she said into his chest.

Jack felt his own band on his finger with his thumb. He thought about when they went to pick out the rings together, not sure what they wanted. They didn't have a lot of money. They settled on simple, matching gold bands. "Sorry I said it was just a band."

"OK," Julie said. "Should we let the park rangers know we lost it here?"

Jack thought about it for a second. "We'll come back later when there aren't so many people around. If we don't find it then, we'll let them know. Let's go into town and take care of things and then come back."

CHAPTER FOUR

J ack drove on the two-lane highway bordered by fields and farms that led them north to Pelican Rapids. The windows were down and they had the radio turned up for their car party drive into town. They all sang along to the song at the top of their lungs. Julie and Lynn shook their heads, their hair blowing in the wind swirling in the car. Willy pretended he had a microphone and got into the song. Jack smiled as he watched his family. This was going to be a good vacation.

"Pelican Rapids. Population two thousand three hundred and seventy-four," Lynn read from the green sign as they passed it.

"Mom, how many people live in Minneapolis?" Willy asked.

"I don't know, maybe Minneapolis is half a million, the whole Twin Cities is over three million."

"Pelican Rapids is a lot smaller," Willy responded. "A lot smaller."

Jack turned the music down as they entered the city limits. They drove by the electric coop, the Dairy Queen, a grocery store, gas station, an elementary school, and the high school. "Hey, look. Fast-food, it can't be that small of a town," Jack said as they drove by a Burger King. He stopped at a red light. The first traffic light they'd encountered.

Ahead a few blocks was another stoplight. "Looks like a two stoplight town. That's pretty small." Julie said.

Jack pulled ahead when the light turned green, drove ahead for half of a block and pulled over to park at the curb. "On your right is the world's largest pelican."

"What?" Willy asked. He turned to look out the window.

Between two old brick store buildings, they saw a giant white pelican with an orange bill. It stood towering over the people who walked around it on a concrete platform that jutted out into a small river at the base of a spillway. Foam licked at its orange webbed feet.

"Hey, cool," Lynn said.

"Let's go," Julie said. "We'll walk around, check out the town and get the groceries, fishing licenses, supplies, and go back to the cabin for our first vacation dinner and a campfire."

"And look for the ring," Jack added.

"Can we go see the pelican first?" Willy asked.

"Sure, let's go," Julie said.

Jack held Julie's hand as they walked down the sidewalk. He rubbed her finger where her ring had been. They had to find a way to get the ring back. The kids ran up ahead to find their way around the buildings to get to the park where the pelican stood guard.

"Seems like a nice, little town," Julie said.

"I don't think I could live here, but not a bad place to vacation," Jack answered. He could already feel some of the stress leaving his body as he slowed to enjoy the surroundings.

Across the street were a cafe and a hardware store. Ahead was a Somali cafe, and a Mexican food truck was parked on the street. Pretty diverse for a small town. The summer vacationers had the drug store offering kayak rentals, knick-knacks, and t-shirts.

They rounded the last building and headed for the park. The kids were already out of sight. Jack searched for them and spied them on the playground. The park was busy with kids on a playground, couples sitting in the shade, people walking across a bridge that spanned a pond.

Julie stopped short and squeezed Jack's hand. She pulled him to a stop. He followed her gaze to see why she stopped.

Ahead of them a twenty-something man yelled at an older man and shoved him. The younger man was about five foot ten, wore a white tank top and jeans. Wiry, his muscles rippled across his bare, tattooed arms. He had a scraggly beard, and long, greasy hair covered with a dirty ball cap, worn backward.

The older man was shorter by a couple of inches, a little stooped. He'd been strong in his younger days. He had broader shoulders, large forearms stuck out of his polo shirt sleeves. He held on firmly to his cane.

The younger man yelled, "I told you old man, quit asking questions and get out of town."

The older man stumbled, his cane slipped on the grass and he fell to a knee.

Jack positioned himself instinctively between the fight and Julie. "Go find the kids." He pointed towards the playground. "I got this."

The young man grabbed the cane and pushed the old man down in the grass.

"Hey!" Jack yelled. "Take it easy there." He walked quickly towards the men. Reflexively, he reached his hand behind his back. His gun wasn't there. It was in the lockbox in the cabin. He held his arms out from his sides, his palms out, showing he had nothing in his hands.

"Fuck off. This is between us," the young man answered. He held the cane in one hand, waving it in the air.

A couple of people stopped and held their phones out, recording the incident.

"I think you've won, whatever your argument was," Jack replied. He kept his voice calm. He took another step forward to get between the young man and the old man on the ground.

"This doesn't involve you." The young man raised the cane over his head.

Jack took two quick steps towards the young man and got within the arc of the swing. He turned, grabbed the man's arm as it swung down over his shoulder, and pushed his hip into the man. He used the momentum to flip him over his shoulder and onto the ground.

The man exhaled with a grunt when he hit the ground. Jack kept a hold of the arm, placed a foot on his chest, twisted his wrist, freeing the cane from the man's grasp, and pushed the tip of the cane into his throat. He continued to hold the wrist with the other hand, bending back the man's thumb at an unnatural angle.

The man twisted and swore at him, but Jack kept the pressure on.

"Settle down," Jack ordered.

"Hey, what's going on?" A twenty-something woman appeared and knelt by the old man on the ground. "You OK?" she asked.

"Yeah," he answered. "Thanks."

She helped the old man into a sitting position on the grass. "Put your phones away," she said to the people standing around them. "There's nothing going on here."

The young man croaked with the cane pressed against his throat. "Angie, get this clown off of me."

"It's Angela."

She circled to where Jack could see her. Wearing jean shorts, a yellow tank top, and gold sandals, she looked strong, like a gymnast. The muscles in her arms, shoulders and legs were well-defined.

Jack watched her while he controlled the bully. Not short, not tall, dark hair, skin that tanned easily. She seemed interested, confident. She kept her distance.

She reached behind her back, pulled out a badge, and showed it to Jack. "Clint, what have you been up to now?" she asked the man on the ground.

The woman was a cop. That surprised Jack. And the bully had a name. Jack responded, "Clint here was beating up on the gentleman and pushed him down in the grass. I thought I should help and Clint ended up on the ground when he tried to hit me with the cane."

The old man limped over and stood next to Angela. "You doing OK?" she asked.

"I'm fine. We had a little disagreement." He coughed a few times. "Can I have my cane back?"

"You going to behave, Clint? Can I let you up now?" Jack asked.

"Yep," he croaked.

Jack lifted the tip of the cane from Clint's throat and held it out for the old man. Then he released Clint's wrist, raised his foot and stepped back, ready to react if Clint tried anything.

Clint got up, shook out his arm, rubbed his throat and glared at Jack and the old man.

"Everybody OK here?" Angela asked. "Anybody want to press any charges today?"

They all shook their heads. "I'd ask you to shake hands, but I think it's better if you just get on your bike, go home, and cool off, Clint. I'll stay here and talk with these gentlemen."

Clint walked towards the parking lot, looked back over his shoulder and then continued over to his motorcycle.

"Let's go sit at that picnic table in the shade and have a little talk." Angela pointed towards the table. "I'm Chief Angela Rancone with the Pelican Rapids police department. She held onto the old man's arm and guided him to the table.

Chief? Jack thought. He sat down across the table from Angela and the old man.

Angela started the conversation. "You sure you're OK?" she asked the old man.

"Yes, I'll be fine."

"Let's start with introductions and where we're from and what we're doing in Pelican Rapids."

The old man coughed into his hand. He dug in his pocket and pulled out a cough drop or something and put it in his mouth. "I'm Cyrus." He looked at Jack. "Thanks for the help." He stuck out his hand.

Jack grabbed his hand and shook it. He was surprised by the size and strength of his grip. The man had a large hand, rough skin. "Glad I could help."

Cyrus continued. "I'm from Chicago. Just visiting. I've been here for the summer and plan to be here for a few more weeks."

"Where are you staying?" Angela asked.

"I have a camper out at Maplewood State Park."

"Sounds good. It's beautiful out there."

"It is," Cyrus replied.

She turned to Jack. "And you? Cop or military?"

Jack started to answer, but stopped when he saw Julie approaching with the kids. He gave her a little wave, letting her know she should stay away, that he was OK. "Why do you think I'm a cop?" he asked.

"I saw how you handled Clint. You've done it before."

"You're good." Jack pulled his credentials out of his back

pocket, opened them and slid them across the table. Angela looked them over while Jack continued. "I'm Special Agent Jack Miller, from Minneapolis. That's my wife and kids. We just got here this morning. We're here vacationing for a couple of weeks until school starts. Staying at a cabin on the south end of South Lida."

"Just here for pleasure? No business?" Angela asked.

"Just pleasure, two weeks of vacation with the family."

Angela folded the credentials and slid them back to Jack. "Two weeks, must be nice. A great way to finish the summer before the kids go back to school."

Jack smiled. "I might go crazy not working for two weeks, but I think we'll find plenty to do. The afternoon has started out a little more exciting than I was expecting."

"Plenty to do. Hope you find other exciting things to do." Angela pulled some postcards out of her pocket and gave one to Cyrus and one to Jack. "We have a street dance tonight, just past the church over there." She nodded to the buildings lining the north end of the park. "That's why I'm in the park this afternoon. Advertising the street dance. Come check it out."

Angela refocused her attention on Cyrus. "I'm sorry you had a problem today. Can you tell me what it was about?"

"It was just a disagreement that escalated."

"Disagreement about what?"

"It was nothing. He just overreacted. I'm fine."

"Do you know Clint?" Angela asked.

Cyrus shook his head. "No. Maybe saw him ride his motorcycle through town. That's it."

"Clint can be a problem and I know where to find him if you change your mind about pressing charges or if he bothers you anymore." Angela stood up from the table. "Again, I apologize for your introduction to Pelican Rapids. I hope you enjoy your vacations. If you need me, just give the police department a call and ask for me."

"Thanks," Cyrus said.

"Yes, thanks," Jack said. "I have one thing. Maybe you can help me or point me in the right direction."

"I'll try," Angela said.

"We were at the state park swimming beach this morning, me and my family, and my wife's wedding ring slipped off her finger in the lake. We couldn't find it. Not a good first day of vacation."

"Maybe we can help," Angela said. "We have a couple of metal detectors in the city shop for locating property corner pins and things like that. Just stop in and tell them I sent you. The garage is next door to the police station. Just go north on the main street through town and we're a couple of blocks up from the last stoplight, on the right side of the street."

"Thanks. I'd be a hero if I found the ring," Jack said.

"Good luck." She shook Jack's hand and then Cyrus'. "Come join our street dance tonight. End the day on a high note. Bring the family," Angela said. She smiled and walked away towards the main street.

JULIE and the kids came over and joined Jack and Cyrus. After some quick introductions, Julie asked Cyrus, "Are you OK?"

Cyrus frowned and shook his head. "I'm fine. Just wish I wasn't so old, then I'd have shown that punk something." He mimed a left hook and a right jab. Then he winked at the kids. They giggled.

"Can we call somebody for you? Give you a ride?" Julie asked.

"Nope. It's just me here. I'm hanging out for the summer."

"I hate leaving you alone until I'm sure you're OK," Julie said.

Lynn grabbed the postcard from Jack and looked it over. "Hey, there's a street dance tonight. Can we go?"

Willy jumped up and started dancing in the grass at the end of the table. "I love to dance," he said.

Jack checked the time on his phone. "We still have some errands to run and that woman that came over here was the police chief." Jack glanced at Julie. "She said we could stop by the maintenance garage and grab a metal detector."

"I've got one in my truck," Cyrus said.

"Got what?" Jack asked.

"A metal detector. In my truck. I can help you find your ring."

"That settles it," Julie said. "You're coming with us. You help find my ring and we'll feed you dinner." She got up and helped Cyrus stand. "Now, where's your truck?"

Jack shook his head. Not the way he imagined the first day of vacation. So much for family time.

Cyrus pointed towards the parking lot. Julie put her arm in his and they shuffled off in that direction. She looked back at Jack and smiled. "Come on."

CHAPTER FIVE

Otto Hokanson sat at his massive oak desk looking out over the manicured green lawn that ran down to the lake. Fishing boats trolled by on the water. Otto often caught the fisherman pointing and looking up longingly at his giant log home. He watched the fisherman while he puffed on his cigars, a little jealous of them. He hadn't fished for years; instead, he spent his time running the multiple family businesses.

He turned his attention to his children. Clint slouched in a high-backed leather chair to his left, facing the desk. Hanna sat up in the matching chair on his right. They couldn't be any more different. His son was an idiot, partying and acting the tough guy in the community. Hanna was his pride and joy, accounting degree and MBA from the University of Minnesota, the mother of his future grandchild. One day she'd replace him running his companies.

"Clint, what am I hearing? You beat up Cyrus in the park?" Otto ground out his cigar in the giant ashtray on his desk and leaned forward. "Low profile, smart decisions, isn't that what we talked about?"

Clint sat up in the chair. "He's poking around too much, asking too many questions. I wanted to know what he was doing here. I let him know he should leave town. He said no." Clint pulled a new pack of cigarettes from his pocket and smacked it against his hand three times.

Otto shook his head. No smoking around Hanna. She was carrying his first grandchild. Clint put the pack in his pocket.

"But someone stepped in and stopped you, helped Cyrus. And Angela got involved. She called me." Otto took a deep breath and gazed out the window. "That's not low profile."

"The guy knew what he was doing. Put me in a hold, like a cop."

"And you'd know," Hanna said.

"Shut up," Clint said.

Otto cleared his throat to get his kids' attention. "Who was he?"

Clint shook his head. "I don't know. Some guy on vacation. Shorts, white legs, flip-flops. A big guy. In pretty good shape." He stared at Hanna. "But I could take him in a fair fight."

"Right," Hanna said.

Otto picked up the stub of an old cigar and held it between his fingers. "Keep your eyes out for him. If he's a cop, even on vacation, he'll be alert around you as well. Especially now." He added, "and keep your eye out for Cyrus. He's been poking around and I want to know what he's up to. If he's looking for the gold, I want to know where he's looking. And if he gets in the way of our drug business, I want to know."

Binoculars sat on the window ledge. Otto put them to his eyes and scanned the boats. Nobody was catching anything, but it was a beautiful day to be out. He set the binoculars back down and turned to his kids. A couple of weeks and they may be set. A year from now, Hanna's baby would be old enough to crawl on the lawn. Maybe he could let Hanna take over next summer and he could fish.

"Now let's talk business. Hanna, how's month-end looking?"

Hanna reviewed the profit and loss statements for both their legal and illegal businesses. Illegal businesses had been a part of the Hokanson business portfolio since Otto's great-grandfather had started businesses in Pelican Rapids in the early 1900s: farms, logging, and a hardware store, along with gambling, Speakeasies, supplying alcohol during prohibition and using what he learned from smuggling booze from Canada to continue smuggling through the years.

Today, the portfolio included log home building, Midwest fleet delivery services, and telemarketing phone banks, along with retail cedar wood fencing, smuggling from Canada and Otto had been experimenting with drugs: illegal and pharmaceuticals. Besides controlling the regional drug supply, Otto had plans to grow west to the oil fields of North Dakota. Clint had found a supplier of fentanyl, improving their profits with the heroin users.

"We had a loss last night. A delivery of pharmaceuticals got lost in a sting on Amtrak in St. Paul," Hanna said. She stared at Clint, "and a sample supply of heroin and fentanyl from a new supplier in Chicago."

Otto pointed his finger at Clint. "That's what you should be spending your time on. Figure out how the sting happened and find us alternatives for getting the drugs from Chicago and Minneapolis." He stabbed his finger into the top of the oak desk. "Figure this out. We have two weeks to get ready for the festival."

Coming around the desk, Otto put out his hand and helped Hanna to her feet. He put his hand on her belly. "Everything going OK? You feeling OK? Getting enough rest?"

Hanna smiled and nodded. "I'm fine."

Hanna decided she wanted to be a mother and found a strong, good looking local boy to sleep with. When she found out she was pregnant, Otto made sure she had the father sign some papers, leaving him free of any child support as long as he made no claims on the child. The young man was happy to sign, both because he didn't want to be responsible for a child, and he wanted to distance himself from any problems with the Hokanson family.

"Is he active?"

"Dad, it might be a girl."

"It might be," Otto said. "But, I'm betting it's a boy." He held her hand in both of his and looked into her eyes. "Go get some rest. Clint and I are going to talk."

OTTO GRABBED a cigar from the humidor on his desk and led the way out onto the deck. They sat in chairs facing the lake. "I want you to find out who this guy is. Is he a cop? Where's he staying? What's he doing here?"

"OK, I'll see what I can find out." Clint tore open the end of his pack of cigarettes, tapped one out, lit it and then held the lighter out to light Otto's cigar. They both inhaled and blew smoke up towards the sky. "What about Cyrus?"

"Leave him alone as long as he leaves us alone. The festival is Labor Day weekend. I don't want anything to jeopardize that," Otto said. "We going to be ready?"

"The alcohol is lined up. We're finalizing the heroin, fentanyl mix. The word is out that we've got the mix. I've given out some samples. They know they can get what they want at the ranch at a great price." Clint sucked on his cigarette again and blew out a stream of smoke. "And everyone knows we're the only supplier. I've scared everyone else out of the county."

"And you have enough supply?" Otto asked. "We lost some the other night according to Hanna."

"Don't worry," Clint answered. "We've got plenty and another shipment is coming through in a couple of nights. We'll be ready for the festival. But, if we're going to expand in the future to the oil patch, we need to find some alternatives."

Otto walked over to the railing. "Let's get through this weekend and then we'll figure it out."

"What about the gold?" Clint asked.

"I'm beginning to wonder if there is any gold left," Otto answered.

"But why else would Cyrus be here? You said he's never been back since he left as a kid."

It looked like there was some action out on a boat on the lake. Otto watched the fisherman land a nice Northern. It would be nice to join them on the lake. Next summer, once the drug business was up and running, he could retire. If there was gold and they found the gold they could all retire. "Cyrus is old and sick. I think he's just tying up some loose ends," Otto said. He turned to Clint. "Focus on the drug business, success at the festival next weekend, and find out who this cop is. And keep an eye on Cyrus in case our gold is hidden out there somewhere."

CHAPTER SIX

The state park beach was a little less crowded now. It was getting closer to suppertime and not as hot as it was earlier in the afternoon. Cyrus sat at a picnic table with Lynn, Jack, and Julie. Willy stood next to him while Cyrus demonstrated how the metal detector worked by throwing a couple of coins on the ground. Willy swept the circular end of the detector back and forth over the coins, the beep growing in strength as the detector coil neared the coins.

"Why can't we use a magnet?" Lynn asked.

"Not all metal is magnetic," Cyrus explained. "Coins and gold rings, don't have steel in them, so they're not magnetic. But the metal detector detects all kinds of metal."

Julie turned to Jack, held his face in her hands and kissed him. "Go find my ring and be my hero," she said.

"Yuck," Willy said. "Let's go, guys." He headed towards the water with the metal detector. Lynn followed with the scoop. It was a giant slotted spoon on the end of a broomstick; a strainer with a long wooden handle.

"Just a second. Let's get our bearings." Jack walked to the spot he marked on shore earlier in the afternoon. He looked back towards land and then out across the lake, lining up his path to the water with a cabin across the lake.

"Now remember, Jack," Cyrus yelled. "When you think you've found something, mark the spot with your toe and then Lynn can scoop the spot just ahead of your foot. Slowly. Scoop, raise it to the surface, let the water and sand drain out, and see what you have."

Jack waved a hand to indicate he heard. "Ready, kids?"

"Ready, Dad," Lynn said.

"Let's find Mom's ring," Willy added.

Looking at the cabin across the lake, Jack walked out into the water, counting his steps until he reached the spot he figured Julie was standing. "X marks the spot, Willy. Start sweeping."

Willy slowly swept the metal detector back and forth over the bottom of the lake. The control box and speaker were on the end of the arm above the water. The speaker squawked on the third sweep.

"OK, there's something there. Zero in on it and I'll mark it," Jack said.

After a couple of shorter sweeps resulting in stronger beeps, Willy rested the detector over a spot on the bottom of the lake. A constant beep emanated from the speaker. Jack stepped over and slid his right foot to the ring of the detector. "OK, I got it marked. You can move it away now."

Willy took a couple of steps back.

"OK, Lynn," Jack said. "Your turn. Carefully dig a deep scoop here at the end of my foot, don't take off a toe, and then slowly raise it up and we'll see what we've got."

Lynn executed the steps as Jack directed. She raised the scoop of sand up through the water. Sand ran out of the holes in the metal scoop. Jack reached over and grabbed the stick and gently sloshed it around to wash out remaining sand.

"Did we get anything?" Willy asked.

"There's something in there," Lynn said.

Jack reached into the scoop and grabbed a couple of small stones that were too big to fit through the holes in the scoop. He tossed them into the water. "A couple of rocks," he said. "But there's something else here."

"Is it the ring?" Lynn asked.

Jack picked up a metal piece and held it up for the kids to see.

"What's that?" Willy asked.

"It's a lead weight used to balance tires," Jack said. He put it in his swimsuit pocket. "Check this spot again, Willy. See if there's anything else here."

Willy slowly swept the spot by Jack's foot and it beeped. They repeated the steps and Lynn raised the scoop again.

"The ring?" Lynn asked.

Jack shook his head. He picked out a couple of stones again and then a rusty bolt. "Just a bolt." He put it in his pocket. "Check it again."

Willy swept the area by Jack's foot. There weren't any beeps.

Jack looked back at Julie to gauge his location. "Anything?" she yelled. Jack gave her a thumbs-down.

He turned back to the kids and then looked out across the lake at their cabin. "Willy, start sweeping from where you're at and walk straight towards the cabin there across the lake."

Willy started his job with a serious look on his face. Lynn followed as they slowly worked their way south. They moved about five yards and the detector squawked again. "Dad, there's something here."

"OK. Zero in on the spot and I'll come mark it."

Jack marked the location again with his foot and Lynn did her job with the scoop. When the scoop came to the surface, Jack spied a couple of items in the basket. He picked out the first one. It was an old dog license tag. "Hey, kids. Look at this." He handed the tag to Willy and Lynn joined him to see it. While they were busy, Jack picked the ring out of the basket and put it in his pocket. He didn't want to just give it to Julie now. He wanted to make a big deal out of it.

"This is cool, Dad," Willy said.

"We'll look at it when we get back to the beach," Jack said. "Let's keep looking for the ring. Check this spot again and we'll see what we find." He took the license from Willy and put it in his pocket with the other metal pieces.

They checked the spot by Jack's foot with no results. They swept an area in about a ten-foot circle from where Jack stood without any more finds.

"Let's go back, guys. We should wrap things up if we want to get to the street party." Jack exchanged the dog license with Willy for the metal detector and they walked back through the lake towards the beach.

When they reached shore, Willy ran up to the table where Julie and Cyrus sat. "You found it?" Julie exclaimed.

"No," Willy replied. "Sorry." He stood at the end of the table with Cyrus and Julie on either side. "But, look what we found" He placed the dog license on the table between them. It was a metal tag with information stamped on it. "It says, Nineteen Forty-two, Dog Tax, Pelican Rapids, number one hundred and seven."

"Can I see it?" Cyrus asked. He held it in his hand and rubbed it with a finger. "Nineteen Forty-two. That's pretty old. I wonder how that got here."

Jack and Lynn joined them at the table. "We found some other metal too, but no ring." Jack placed the contents of his pocket on the table. "Sorry, Jules. We can try again."

"We'll find it, Mom," Lynn said, and hugged her.

"You proved it works," Julie said. She stood up and put

her arms around Jack and stared into his eyes. "Thanks for looking."

"We'll find it." Jack kissed her.

"We better go take care of Vince and get ready for the street dance," Julie said. "Thank you all for looking. And thanks for the metal detector, Cyrus. We'll try again."

CHAPTER SEVEN

The sun was still shining when they got to the park in Pelican Rapids, but the one and two-story buildings lining Main Street, and the trees along the edge of the park were starting to cast their shadows. The carnival filled the park with vendors selling food, crafts, face painting, and temporary tattoos. Smoke from the grilling pits where turkey legs and breasts roasted, floated over their heads. Families milled about. There were kiddie rides in the parking lot where the shrieks and screams of children filled the air.

Jack and Julie walked hand-in-hand. He felt her naked ring finger between his fingers. He felt bad not giving her the ring at the park, but he decided he wanted to make putting the ring back on her finger a special moment. The time had to be right.

The kids walked ahead of them on either side of Cyrus, each holding a hand. Lynn carried Cyrus' cane like a baton. Jack squeezed Julie's hand to get her attention. She looked at him. He nodded at the kids and Cyrus. "What do you think?" he asked.

Julie smiled. "It's cute."

"Yeah, cute." Jack wondered how long Cyrus was going to be around. This family vacation wasn't starting out as he'd planned. Once they were sure Cyrus was OK, Julie would be comfortable and Jack could take him back to where he was staying.

The group made it to the party in the park. "I think we owe Cyrus dinner for the metal detector," Julie said.

"Is everyone hungry?" Jack asked. He pulled some bills from his pocket and handed them to Lynn. "Let's go get us some plates of food." He studied the sign at the food tent. "Looks like turkey legs, turkey sandwiches, beans, chips, and ice cream sandwiches. I hope everyone likes turkey." He turned to Julie. "Why don't you two find us a place to sit. We'll find you."

Willy and Lynn ran to the food tent to get in line. Jack walked over to join them. Willy and Lynn rambled on about the day, what food they wanted to eat. Jack observed the crowd. He couldn't turn it off. He was always checking out the people around him. Nothing seemed out of the ordinary. People laughed, kids played, some men's club ran the barbecue pits. Nobody seemed out of place. Jack had to relax and enjoy his vacation.

After working their way through the line and getting the plates of food, Jack and the kids joined Julie and Cyrus at a table by the old mill pond in the middle of the park. They passed around the plates of food. "Looks good," Julie said. "Thanks for getting it."

"Enjoy," Jack said. "I'm starving."

"This pond here is where I learned how to swim when I was a kid," Cyrus said.

"Really?" Julie asked. "Not in a lake?"

"Nah, we lived in town, so I'd bike over here for lessons in the summer. Mom wanted to make sure we all knew how to swim since we were going to be around the lakes so much."

Cyrus stopped for a second and coughed. Once he recovered, he continued. "Now there's a public pool in town. Nobody wants to swim in a cold, dirty pond."

A few ducks swam around on the pond. Kids stood on the shore tossing pieces of bread to them. Cyrus stuck the plastic tip of a swisher sweet cigar in his mouth. Julie shook her head. Cyrus smiled and left it unlit.

"How long did you stay around here?" Jack asked.

Taking the cigar out of his mouth, Cyrus answered. "I left when I graduated from high school. Joined the Navy. Always liked boats and felt comfortable on the water."

"You knew how to swim," Jack added.

Cyrus smiled.

"And you live in Chicago?" Julie asked.

Cyrus nodded. "Yep, we," he paused. "I live in Chicago. My wife, Ruby, and I lived there for a long time." Cyrus closed his eyes, then looked up into the sky. "She died about a year ago."

"I'm so sorry," Julie said.

Cyrus waved it off. "No worries. We lived a long and happy life together. I'm just glad I outlived her. She couldn't have lived without me." He winked at Julie.

Julie reached across the table and squeezed Cyrus' hand.

Jack watched Julie and how she cared for Cyrus. He thought about what a lucky guy he was. "Did you have any kids?" Jack asked.

"Nope. We weren't blessed in that way. But we were kind of the neighborhood grandparents."

"I can see that," Jack said. "Our kids have taken to you."

There was an awkward silence and then Jack asked, "so what brings you to Pelican Rapids now?"

Cyrus coughed and wiped his mouth. "I'm getting old. Thought I should come back and see the place. Never got Ruby here. If I was going to do it, now was the time. This is the best time of year here. Wouldn't want to visit in the winter."

"You're right about that." Jack scanned the crowd while he ate. "We have the extremes in weather."

As they finished eating, Cyrus told the kids some stories about living in Chicago, about how it was different than Minneapolis, more people, and traffic and how it had changed since he moved there when he was done with the Navy. They talked about the Bears and the Vikings, the Twins and the Cubs.

Music started from the street outside of the park, on the other side of the Catholic church, past the playground. The boom of the bass vibrated their plastic cups on top of the picnic table. Then a woman started to sing. It sounded like a country western song.

People made their way towards the source of the music, drawn like mice to the pied piper.

"Dad, let's go to the street dance," Lynn said.

Willy drummed the top of the table to the beat with his plastic fork and spoon.

"Should we go?" Julie asked. "You up to visit the dance, Cyrus?"

Cyrus pushed himself up from the picnic table. "Try and stop me. I didn't come here for the turkey. Dancing is one thing Ruby and I did every weekend."

Julie grabbed Jack's hand and pulled him up from the table. "Come on. If Cyrus can dance, so can you."

Jack stood up, held Julie's hand, and spun her in a circle. "I might surprise you."

THE BAND FINISHED their country western song by the time Cyrus, Jack, and his family made it to the street. One end was a dead end. The stage and speakers were at that end. The other end of the street, the second stoplight in town, about two blocks from the stage, was closed off to traffic with barricades.

Jack felt himself grow a little tense, and he started to search the crowd. Inside the barricades, there were vendors selling snow-cones, water, sodas, and beer. Within the two blocks was a conglomeration of people representing summer in Otter Tail County. There were local families with their kids: white, Hispanic and Somali. The older locals sat in chairs along the curbs, wearing straw hats and baseball caps from the local co-op or farm and feed stores in the area. The vacationers wore flip-flops, t-shirts and most were sunburned.

He spied Clint and kept him within view. After grabbing some snow-cones and beverages, Jack and the kids found Julie and Cyrus standing along the curb about thirty yards from the stage. Jack handed Cyrus a beer and Julie a water. They clinked them together in a toast. The kids were each licking the rainbow ice snow cones with sticky juice running down their chins and hands.

Jack leaned into Cyrus. "I see your friend from the park, Clint, is here. He's back there towards the beer garden." He flicked his head in the direction of the vendors.

"I hope he doesn't ask me to dance," Cyrus answered. Then he started laughing, which turned into coughing and he bent over while he hacked.

A long drumroll brought their attention to the stage. A man walked out with a microphone in his hand. "Welcome everyone," he said. "Are you all ready to have a good time?"

The crowd cheered.

Cyrus coughed and said, "Asshole," into his hand.

"Tonight is for you. My name is Otto Hokanson and I am up here to welcome you to this street dance brought to you by Hokanson Enterprises. We hope you have a great time. If you're around in two weeks, you're all invited to join us at the

Hokanson Ranch where we have some big-time country artists lined up to play for you. Discount tickets are for sale for the Fall Music Festival at a couple of booths back there," he pointed towards the other end of the street. "You don't want to hear me talk. Let's get the band back up here. You all have a great time tonight!" Otto clapped his hands over his head and waved to the crowd. Then he walked off the stage.

THE BAND STARTED PLAYING AGAIN. This time it was a bluegrass number. Cyrus handed Jack his cane. "Mind if I ask your lovely bride for a dance?"

Jack took the cane and replied. "See if she can keep up."

Cyrus led Julie by the hand through the crowd. He kissed her hand, bowed his head slightly and started to move. His footsteps were short, but he guided Julie through moves in time with the music.

"Dad, he's a good dancer," Lynn said.

Willy added, "So is Mom."

Jack smiled. "They're pretty good out there. I have some competition." He took another drink of his beer and scanned the crowd. He caught himself and told himself to relax. He did have his family in a town he didn't know, with people he didn't know, so his senses were on alert.

He spotted Clint drinking back at the beer garden with a group of what looked like local guys, trying to hit on three young, blonde women.

A sticky hand grabbed Jack's. "We want to dance," Lynn said.

Jack grabbed Willy's hand in his other. "Let's go show those two how to dance."

The five of them all formed a circle in the street and danced with each other, the kids showing Cyrus some fancy footwork and Cyrus spinning them around in circles. Jack grabbed Julie, one of her hands in his, the other on the small of her back as he led her through some steps. As the song drew to a close, he pulled her close and dipped her.

Everyone clapped for the band. The lead singer stepped to the microphone. "You guys are great. It's been a blast to see you all dancing out there. To give you a little rest, we have a special act for you. Gather round and enjoy the show."

Jack stood behind Julie and put his arms around her. The kids stood in front of Cyrus. "You OK to stand here, Cyrus?" Julie asked.

"I'm fine for a while. Why is my cane all sticky?"

Jack shrugged and smiled.

The spotlights on the stage came on and a purple velvet rope lowered from above the stage. "Ladies and gentlemen, prepare to be amazed," the singer said. A slow drumbeat started, joined by a bass and then a piano. A woman dressed in colorful silks and glitter on her skin reflecting the spotlights strode onto the stage. She walked to the rope and climbed it.

"Is that her?" Lynn asked.

"Wow, she's beautiful," Willy said.

Jack watched the woman gracefully climb the rope and spin in time with the music. "I think she kept some secrets from us."

Cyrus started shuffling closer to the stage, Willy and Lynn's hands in each of his. "Let's get a little closer and see what Chief Angela can do."

ANGELA EXECUTED moves that combined grace, strength, and control. At times, the crowd gasped. Other times they applauded. She climbed the rope effortlessly, stopping partway up and performing a move where her body went horizontal, supported only by her arms, then she bent her elbows and tumbled down the ropes a couple of turns before stopping her fall and executing another strength move. This was all in time with the music. The musicians added notes, riffs, and beats that added even more tension to the routine.

"She is strong," Lynn said.

Julie gave Lynn's shoulder a squeeze. "I bet she practices a lot and this keeps her in good shape for her job as well."

Willy poked Jack in the stomach. "What do you do to stay in shape, Dad?"

"Hey." Jack picked Willy up and hugged him. "I'm in pretty good shape. Just not that kind of shape."

Cyrus leaned on his cane and the rest of them stood and watched the routine. A new song started and Angela started her climb again. At the top of the ropes, she twisted it around her body and let go, appearing to float above the stage. The crowd whistled and cheered.

A high-pitched scream filled the air. The band stopped playing and everyone froze. The scream repeated from behind the stage. Jack put Willy down on the ground. "I'll be right back," he said to Julie. He grabbed Cyrus' arm. "Watch these guys," he said. He took off at a run in the direction of the scream.

Jack saw Angela slide down the rope to the stage. She was ahead of him, moving towards the source of the sound behind the stage.

Angela got to the scene just ahead of Jack. She knelt next to a girl, eighteen years old or so. The girl appeared to be passed out, lying on the grass just off the edge of the street. Angela touched the girl's cheek, held open an eye and looked at the pupil. She put a couple of fingers to her neck. "She's breathing," she said. "Her hearts racing. Shallow breathing. I think she's OD'd."

Another girl was sitting nearby on the ground, arms

wrapped around her legs. She was crying and shaking. "They're ... they're dead," she said.

"They?" Jack asked. "Who else is here? Where are they?"

The girl slowly raised her arm and pointed a finger towards some bushes. "Brad. He threw up and stumbled over there and fell down."

Jack hurried over to the bushes. A shirtless young man lay face down in the dirt. "Angela, over here!" He turned the boy over. Angela grabbed his legs to help lay him flat on his back. "He's not breathing," Jack said.

Angela started CPR. She compressed his chest and breathed into the boy's mouth.

Jack went back to the girl sitting on the ground. "Did they take something? What happened?"

"Brad had some drugs. They took some."

Jack returned to Angela. "Sounds like they OD'd."

Angela paused the CPR and glanced back towards the street dance block and then at the group gathered around her. She grabbed Jack's arm and looked him in the eye. "Get one of my officers over here. Tell him we need a squad car or ambulance here now. Narcan's in the car. We'll save this guy and get them moved to the hospital."

Jack hurried through the crowd, dodging around people to find an officer. They ran to the car. Jack grabbed a few packets of Narcan, stuck them in his pockets and ran back to join Angela. She continued the CPR. Jack pulled out a plastic packet and ripped it open. His hands were shaking.

Angela reached out and grabbed the packet from him. She calmly removed the nasal syringe from the package. Then she tilted the young man's head back and injected a dose into one of his nostrils. She rubbed his chest bone with a knuckle. "Brad, wake up," she urged. She pushed on his belly and released. She repeated it.

"He's turning blue," Jack said.

Angela gave Brad another dose of Narcan in his other nostril. She rubbed his chest and patted his cheek. "Come on, Brad. Wake up." She rolled him onto his side and patted his back. "Wake up, Brad."

Brad sucked in a breath, moaned and opened his eyes.

"Brad, you with me?" Angela asked.

"Yeah," he replied groggily.

Angela helped him sit up.

The paramedics were attending to the girl.

The crowd moved out of the way as the ambulance slowly rolled through.

The EMTs from the ambulance had a rolling gurney and a flat board to move the two to the ambulance. They joined Angela and started to check out the young man.

Jack found the girl, the shaking blond teenager. She was wearing a Pelican Rapids High School Vikings t-shirt and sandals. "They're going to be OK," he said. He put out his hand to help her up. "Let's get you to this officer over here and you can tell him what happened and he'll get you home." After getting her to an officer, he found Angela talking with the EMT's at the ambulance. She closed the doors and the ambulance rolled away.

"They going to be OK?" he asked.

Angela nodded. "Yep. Thanks for your help."

Jack thought about how automatically Angela had checked the girl and how she started CPR on the boy. And how calmly she'd administered the Narcan. "You've done this before," he said.

"Too often," she answered. "It's getting worse. Once the summer vacation season's over it'll get a little better. It'll just be the locals to worry about."

Jack studied Angela's face. She was staring ahead without seeing anything. She was sad. She cared. Stuff like this made Jack glad he was an FBI agent and not a cop.

Angela snapped back to the present and looked at Jack. "Thanks again," she said.

"Glad I could help," he said. "Now, I better go find my family. I think the party's over. It's time for us to head back to the cabin."

CHAPTER EIGHT

A loon sang its haunting call across the dark lake. Jack stacked twigs and then bigger sticks in the fire pit and struck a match to light the wad of newspaper he'd put at the bottom. He nursed the flame, gently blowing on it to get it to spread. He thought back to his nights as a boy at Scout camp, where he learned how to make different kinds of fires.

"Not bad for a city boy," Cyrus teased. He sat down in one of the Adirondack chairs facing the fire. He set a bottle of beer on each arm of the chair. "One of these is for you, once you get the fire going."

"Well, that's an incentive." Jack added some more sticks to the fire and blew on the hot coals to get the fire to spread to some of the larger kindling. Smoke swirled and blew into his face. He coughed and squeezed his stinging eyes shut. "I think I can use that beer now." Jack sat in the chair next to Cyrus and accepted a beer. The firelight reflected off Cyrus' glasses in the dark.

Jack held out his bottle and clinked it against Cyrus'. "Thanks. This has been quite a day."

Cyrus took a drink. "This has been quite the start to your vacation. I feel bad that I'm intruding."

"Don't worry about it. You're our guest and we have plenty of room."

The men sat and stared at the fire and drank their beer.

THE SCREEN DOOR on the cabin slammed shut. Julie and the kids walked down the steps carrying marshmallows, graham crackers and chocolate bars for making s'mores. Vince followed them, in case they dropped something.

They joined Jack and Cyrus in the chairs around the fire.

"What did you guys think of Chief Angela's show?" Jack asked.

"She's got to be really strong," Lynn said.

Willy added, "I'd have never guessed a police chief could do that."

"Everybody has some secret skills," Julie said. "Except for Jack." The kids laughed.

"I don't think Dad could climb the rope like Angela did," Lynn said.

Jack and Julie's eyes met. "Everyone OK with what happened in town? Want to talk about it anymore?" Jack asked.

Lynn answered. "We're OK. We talked about it some more with Mom inside." She paused. "It's just kind of sad."

"Why do people use drugs?" Willy asked.

"That, is a good question. We'll have to talk about that one some more later. I don't know if I have a good answer, right now," Jack said. He tossed another log onto the fire. "My skill is fire starter. It's going to be a while until the coals are ready for roasting marshmallows. What should we do until then? Tell ghost stories?"

"No," Willy said. "I won't be able to sleep."

"I have an idea," Cyrus said from the dark, sitting back from the fire. "How about we tell stories of how we think the dog tag you found ended up in the lake?"

"That sounds like a good idea," Julie said. "Since it's your idea, why don't you go first?"

"Can I see the dog tag, Willy?" Cyrus asked.

Willy walked over to Cyrus and removed the dog tag from around his neck. He'd tied some fishing line through the hole in the tag and was wearing it as a necklace. He placed it into Cyrus' open palm. Cyrus closed his hand and held it up to his forehead.

Willy sat in Julie's lap. "What's he doing?" he asked.

"I think the story is coming to him."

Lynn sat in Jack's lap.

Vince lay at Cyrus' feet.

Cyrus lowered his hand from his forehead, opened his fist, blew some smoke from the cigar over the tag, and put the necklace around his own neck. Then he cleared his throat.

"It was a hot summer afternoon in 1942. Picture yourself standing in the grass near the beach, back before it was a state park. It was a forest much like it is today with small farms between the hills." Cyrus took a drink of beer. "Ready? Can you see it?"

Willy nodded, the firelight reflecting in his eyes.

"We're ready," Lynn answered.

Cyrus started to tell his story.

"Crouching in the long grass, Christian looked back."

"Who's Christian?" Willy asked.

"Shh," Julie said. "Cyrus is telling his story."

Cyrus waited a few seconds and continued with his story.

"Christian looked back to judge how far behind him the dogs were. It was hard to tell, but they were still coming. He heard them barking. Christian was gasping from running through the woods and across the fields. He pointed his chin up at the sky to open his throat and inhaled deeply to catch his breath. His heart beat hard in his neck and he thought he heard it as well, drumming in his ears. The lake was a couple of hundred yards away. If he could make it to the lake, he would cross the rock bar to the island. The island wasn't that big. Once he got over or around the island to the other side, he would swim to the west side of the lake and escape. He may not be able to outrun the dogs, but he could out swim them. And if he got to the other side of the lake, the men chasing him would have to follow him or go around the south end of the lake to catch up with him, three, four miles at least. They'd never catch him.

"Christian looked back again, pushed up from his crouch and ran through the tall grass towards the lake. He broke through a row of oak trees and ran across the open ground towards the island, his brown work boots crunching through the dry grass. The lakeshore was ten yards to his left. The rock bar to the island started one hundred yards ahead of him.

"He heard a noise behind him and glanced over his right shoulder. A large black dog broke through the long grass in strong, purposeful bounds. It didn't bark but ran straight towards him, its tongue hanging out of one side of its mouth. Christian didn't think he'd make it to the shallow water at the rock bar. He changed directions and headed left for the lake, splashing into the shallow water just as the dog leaped off of the low bank.

"The dog hit Christian squarely between the shoulder blades knocking him face-first into the water. The shock of the cold lake sucked away his breath. The dog quickly attacked after knocking him down. It bit into his right thigh through his overalls and dragged him back towards the shore, growling deep from its throat as it pulled. Christian clawed at the bottom of the lake with his hands, trying to stop their progress back to shore and pushed up enough to keep his face above the water so he could breathe. The dog kept pulling him towards shore. Christian swung his left leg around, trying to hit the dog, but it had a hold of him too high on his right leg for his left foot to reach it. The dog continued to make progress, its brute strength and determination driving it to pull its prey back to shore.

"Christian reached down with his right arm and grabbed the thin rope collar looped around the dog's neck. He pulled with all his might, trying to twist the dog's head around, wrenching it free from the grip it had on his flesh and overalls. The rope broke. His arm jerked back and the rope collar flew through the air, landing in the water.

"In a last move of desperation, Christian took a deep breath and bent at his waist, his head under the water. He grabbed each of the dog's forelegs in a hand and straightened his body, using the leverage of his weight against the dog's. He arched his back and pulled. The dog's feet slipped from their grip on the sandy bottom and Christian drove the weight of his legs down to the bottom of the lake, pulling the dog's head down below the surface of the water.

"Christian spit water out and stretched his head up for air while he held the struggling dog under the water. He gulped for air and howled as the dog's teeth cut through his skin. Finally, the dog loosened its grip on his leg. Christian stood in the shallow water, each of the dog's forelegs in his hands. The dog thrashed and twisted and broke free of his grip. It ran from the lake, stopped to shake the water from its fur and then ran back the way it had come.

"His leg throbbed. Christian inspected it through the rips in the overalls. It wasn't' bleeding too much. He needed to get going before the men and the other dogs caught up with him. He looked back at the woods and then ran, limping down the beach toward the island."

. . .

THERE WAS a moment of silence and then the questions started.

"Who was he?" Willy asked.

"Who was chasing him?" Lynn asked.

"And why?" Willy added.

"Did he get away?" Lynn asked. "You just made this up? Or how did you get that from the dog tag?"

"Whoa kids, let him answer," Julie said. "That was some story, Cyrus."

Jack watched Cyrus in the dark, the light from the fire dancing across his face. This old man knew more than he shared.

Cyrus stared at the tag in the palm of his hand. "That's the story the tag told me, but it didn't give me all of the answers." He held it out for Willy. "I think we may have a mystery to solve."

Willy took the tag and hung it around his neck.

The loon called across the lake again. An answer came from another loon to the east.

Julie said, "I don't think any of us will top that story. I think we should have some s'mores and go to bed. It's been a long day."

CHAPTER NINE

The sound of clanking dishes in the kitchen woke Jack from his sleep. Somebody was cleaning up after breakfast. Birds sang their songs and a strand of sunlight peaked through the edge of the curtain. Jack reached over to the bedside table and grabbed his phone. 8:54. It had been a long time since he'd slept this late. Maybe he did need this vacation. He stared up at the ceiling fan blowing a gentle breeze over him. Yep, he could get used to vacation. No work worries, sleeping in, hanging out with the kids and Julie.

He threw on some shorts and a t-shirt, stopped in the bathroom, brushed his teeth and walked into the kitchen. Julie was the only one there, standing at the sink, drying the dishes. He walked over to her, wrapped his arms around her and buried his nose in her neck. "Good morning," he said.

"Well, look who's up. Just in time to watch me finish the morning dishes," Julie teased. "I guess you were tired."

"Sorry," Jack mumbled. "I guess I was more tired than I knew." He kissed Julie's neck, grabbed a muffin from the counter and poured himself a cup of coffee. "Thanks for letting me sleep. Where is everybody?"

"They're down on the dock fishing. Cyrus is showing them how. Sounds like they're having fun." The sounds of the kids' voices carried up from the lake.

Jack pushed through the screen door. "I'm going to go see how they're doing."

THE LAKE WAS RELATIVELY QUIET. A few fishermen were out in boats. A jet ski buzzed in the distance. Jack walked down the hill from the cabin to the lake. Vince was wading in the lake up to his belly. The kids stood side-by-side at the end of the dock. Each held a fishing pole in their hands and watched their red and white bobbers floating out in the lake. Cyrus stood behind them, coaching them.

Jack stopped and watched them. He couldn't help but be a little jealous of Cyrus teaching the kids how to fish. This was his vacation. Cyrus seemed recovered. Maybe it was time to get him back to where he was staying at the state park. "Hey guys, how's the fishing?"

"Morning, Dad," Lynn said. "I caught one sunny."

"I caught the biggest fish, so far," Willy said. "Look in the pail."

There was a yellow plastic pail, filled with water, on the dock. Inside there were a few small panfish swimming around.

"Morning, Jack," Cyrus added. "They're doing great. Getting some good practice from the dock. I told them we'd go out in the boat later to try and catch some bigger fish. If it's OK with you."

Jack stepped past Cyrus on the dock. He stood between Lynn and Willy and watched their bobbers. "Yep, we'll have to go after some bigger fish. Those in the bucket are nice, but I don't know if they're big enough to make us a good lunch."

"Or you'll need more," Cyrus added.

"But they're pretty fish, aren't they?" asked Lynn.

"They sure are," Jack said. "You guys figure out how to rig the rods with bobbers and bait by yourselves?"

"Cyrus showed us," Willy said.

Jack just grunted. "You'll show me how?" he asked.

"Sure," Willy said.

The four of them stood on the dock and watched the bobbers, waiting for another fish to bite.

"JACK!" Julie yelled down from the cabin. "Chief Angela is here to see you."

Julie and Angela stood up by the cabin, waiting for Jack to come up. Angela was dressed for business in her police chief uniform. She wore pants with black boots, a blue, short-sleeved button-up shirt. The lump of the Kevlar vest was visible underneath. She held a steaming cup of coffee in her hand. Sunglasses shaded her eyes. Her dark hair was held back in a ponytail.

"Wonder what she's doing here?" Jack said.

"Can we keep fishing, dad?" Lynn asked.

"Sure." Jack poured his remaining coffee in the lake and stepped by Cyrus on the dock. "See if you can catch us some lunch. And don't fall in."

"I think I'll join you," Cyrus said. "I need to sit down for a little while and another cup of coffee would be good."

Vince ran ahead up the hill to check out their visitor. Jack and Cyrus followed. "Hey, Chief," Jack greeted her with a wave.

Angela waved back and waited for Jack and Cyrus to get up the grassy hill.

Jack made it to the top. "I should be in pretty good shape after this vacation going up and down this hill. It's not that big, but it's big enough to give me a little workout." He glanced back at Cyrus. He was making progress. "So, Chief, what's up? Looks like you're working so I'm guessing you're here for something."

"Can we sit on the porch and talk?"

"Jack, why didn't you help Cyrus up the hill?" Julie asked.

"He's OK," Jack said. "You OK, Cyrus?" he asked in a louder voice.

Cyrus waved and continued walking up the hill with his cane.

Jack held open the screen door for Julie and Angela, entered and let it slam shut behind him. Julie asked if everyone wanted some more coffee. "Cyrus, you want some coffee?" she yelled to him. He gave her a thumbs-up.

"You gave us a little surprise last night with your ropes act, Chief," Jack said.

Angela pushed her sunglasses up onto the top of her head. "Just something I do to keep in shape. It's more fun than running. And you can call me Angela."

"You must've been doing it for a while," Julie said. "You were flawless. It was artistic and athletic."

Cyrus shuffled onto the porch and joined the group at the table. He coughed and sat down, wheezing a little. "I forgot my meds are in my camper," he said.

"We'll get you back there to get those," Julie said. "Sorry, we interrupted your story, Angela."

"I was saying the ropes was something I started when I was younger. Enjoyed it, so I keep doing it. It's kind of fun to show off for the people in town. Show them I'm more than just a cop," Angela said.

Cyrus said, "Not something you'd expect your Chief of Police to do."

"How're the girl and boy from last night?" Julie asked.

Angela held her coffee cup in both hands and slid it in

small circles on the tabletop. "The girl will be OK. He didn't make it."

Nobody said anything for a couple of beats.

"I'm so sorry," Julie said.

"I thought you'd saved him," Jack said.

"So did I," Angela replied.

"I hate drugs," Cyrus said. "They cause nothing but problems in Chicago and even here. Did you know him?"

Angela nodded. "Who don't I know in Pelican Rapids? It's a small town."

Jack held out the pot to see if anyone needed a refill. Everyone was good. He poured himself a cup. Cyrus chewed on the plastic tip of a fresh cigar. Vince patrolled around the table, looking for dropped crumbs. "So, Chief, why are you here this morning?" Jack asked. "You heard we brewed good coffee or you check on all visitors? We're a little out of your jurisdiction."

Angela's eyes hardened and she stared directly into Jack's eyes. "Drugs are coming into Otter Tail County, into Pelican Rapids. We've had plenty of issues related to them, but this is the first death. I don't want another one. But, we can hardly make a dent in this alone." Angela paused. "I'm not sure who I can trust. There are some powerful forces at work here and I'm hoping you'll help me take a look at this. An outside perspective from the law enforcement angle."

Jack answered. "I appreciate the predicament you're in, but I'm one FBI agent on vacation. I don't know a lot about drugs and trafficking, it's not my area. I can connect you with our field office liaison in Fargo, maybe the DEA or BCA."

"That will take too long. We're winding down the summer tourist season here and I was just hoping you could come in, take a look at some of our reports and offer some suggestions on areas to look at. I want to end the summer on a plus, not a big minus."

"How about the county sheriff?" Jack asked.

Angela shook her head. "Like I said, there are some forces at work here and I'm not sure who I can trust."

"What are these forces you mention?" Jack asked.

"I'd rather discuss it in my office."

Jack liked Angela. She was young, smart, tough, wanted to do what was right. She cared about her town. Julie nudged Jack under the table. He glanced at her and she gave a quick shake of her head. He knew she didn't want him jumping into this. They were on vacation.

The kids entered the porch carrying their bucket of fish. Water sloshed over the edges. "Wait until you see what Lynn caught," Willy said.

"Hey, Ms. Angela!" Lynn said. "You were great last night." She sat on the bench by the Chief.

Angela replied, "Thank you. It was a lot of fun. What did you catch?"

"We caught a few panfish, right Cyrus?" Lynn got up and brought the bucket over and set it at Angela's feet. Then she reached in and held up a big fish. "And this one." She used both hands to hold it up. It was the length of her arm and almost as big around as her head.

"Wow," Angela said. "That is one nice bass."

Willy was jumping up and down. "Can we keep him?"

Cyrus held out his hand. "Can I see him?" Lynn held the fish out and Cyrus grabbed it by the lower lip. "A nice sport fish like this one, the bass, is usually catch and release. Catch them for fun and then let them go so they can keep growing bigger and you can catch them again." He carefully put the fish back in the bucket.

Willy and Lynn both looked disappointed.

"But don't worry. I'm sure you kids and your dad will catch some fine Northerns or Walleye, maybe some Crappies on vacation and have nice fish dinners the next couple of weeks," Cyrus said. "Willy, before you dump the fish back in the lake why don't you show Angela what else you found in the lake."

Willy stepped over to Angela and pulled the necklace with the dog license over his head. He held it out to her. "We found this old dog license tag. It says it's from 1942."

Angela held it in her hand.

"Last night we were telling stories about how we thought it might have ended up in the lake." Willy pointed across the lake. "We found it over there at the beach."

"That is so cool. Weren't you looking for your mom's wedding ring too?"

"'They looked," Julie said. "And found that and some other metal things, but not the ring. We'll have to look again."

Angela turned to Willy "You know, if you're in town we have a room with old records in it. You could probably find out whose dog this belonged to and solve part of your mystery."

"Can we go now?" Willy asked.

Cyrus added, "I have to get back to town and leave you all to your vacation."

Angela glanced at Jack. "And a quick stop at the police station to look at our issue while they search the records?"

Jack got up from the table and kissed Julie on the forehead. "A quick stop," he said.

Julie shrugged.

"Go dump your catch in the lake," Jack said. "Cyrus and I will meet you at the car." He looked at Angela. "We'll see you at the station."

CHAPTER TEN

O tto sat at the table on the deck overlooking the lake. The deck umbrella cast its shadow over him while he read the Minneapolis newspaper, the Star Tribune. The Twins were on a run, they were making a season of it. They finally had some pitchers. He drank some coffee and turned the page. Hanna joined him at the table. "Good morning, Daddy."

"Hey, sweetheart. Can I pour you some coffee or some juice?"

"Juice, please."

Otto poured the orange juice for her and set it in front of her. He smiled. "Are you doing OK giving up junk food and cutting back on caffeine for that little one?"

"I've never eaten so healthy, and felt so miserable," Hanna said with half a smile.

"Is your brother up yet?"

"I heard him in the shower when I walked by. He should be out in a minute." She sipped the juice. "Did the Twins win?"

"Extra innings. They pulled it out."

Hanna reached for the business section of the paper and read that while she drank her juice.

Clint walked onto the deck, his wet hair combed back. "Twins won. I heard it on my way home last night." He grabbed the sports section and plopped down in the chair across from Otto. He reached for the coffeepot and poured himself a cup. "What's for breakfast?"

Otto glanced back at the house and nodded. Kate emerged from the house carrying a tray with their plates of food. She wore khaki shorts and a crisp green button-up shirt with short sleeves, her uniform. Her dark hair was pulled back in a short ponytail. Otto was happy with how she was working out. She'd been with them for the summer. Coming to them from some small farm in the middle of South Dakota, she wanted to earn money working for a year before going to college. In addition to cooking and cleaning, she'd be an au pair for Hanna's baby when it was born.

Clint started eating as soon as Kate set his plate in front of him.

"You pig," Hanna said.

Otto waited until they all had their food, poured himself some more coffee and asked the question. "What happened last night?"

Hanna shrugged.

Clint swallowed a bite of his eggs and looked up. "What?"

Leaning forward, Otto locked eyes with Clint. "I asked, what happened last night?"

"There was a street dance in town last night," Clint answered.

"I know there was a street dance last night. I'm talking about the overdoses at the dance and the death," Otto said.

"Death?" Clint leaned forward.

Otto had his attention now. "Yes. Some kids OD'd last night. One died."

"Who was it?"

"I didn't get a name yet. A local high school boy," Otto said.

Hanna joined the conversation. "That's terrible." She poured herself another glass of juice. "Was it our product?"

"Who cares?" Clint asked.

Otto rapped his knuckles on the table. "Clint, listen. Answer her questions and learn something."

Hanna readjusted her chair, angling it to more directly face Clint. "If it's not our product, where did they get it? Do we have competition? Is someone trying to move into our territory?" She cleared her throat. "If it's our product, did they OD because they took too much or is something wrong with our product? Since someone OD'd and someone died, who will they trace the product back to?"

Clint shifted in his chair and leaned back. "I think it was our product."

Otto massaged his forehead while he got his emotions under control and his thoughts together. When he was ready, he turned and faced Clint. "We have a lot of cash coming in from these sales. More than Hanna can explain with our current portfolio of businesses. But with the Festival we'll be able to launder the cash we have, make more money and be set for repeating it next year." He paused, staring into Clint's eyes. Clint looked down and Otto continued, "But we can't have anything interrupt the flow of cash. We can't have anything bring scrutiny to our corporation. And the festival has to come off successfully. We all have our piece in this that we have to perform."

"I got it," Clint said. "We have some more drugs coming in. I'll check the product we have mixed so far and let my sellers out there know that they should dump anything they're still holding from last week's supply."

Otto answered, "Now you're thinking. I'll find out the

cause of death if they can determine that. Make sure we have good stuff. That's one reason we can keep other suppliers out of here. Trust. People trust our product is good."

The three of them sat at the table. A jet ski went by, interrupting the silence.

"Finish your breakfast," Otto said. "Let's meet back here for a late lunch. We'll have some answers to those questions and Hanna will update us on the plans for the Festival."

CHAPTER ELEVEN

A sunny morning, still cool, they drove with the windows down, enjoying the fresh air. Jack and Cyrus sat in front, Willy and Lynn sat in the back seat. Jack maintained a two-car gap behind Angela as they followed her into town. "We'll stop at the police station, see how I can help Angela. You guys see what you can find out about the dog license," Jack said loud enough for everyone to hear over the noise of the wind blowing in the windows. He tilted his head towards Cyrus. "Then we'll find your car, get you back to your vacation."

Cyrus smiled and nodded.

"Cyrus is coming back to the lake, isn't he?" Willy asked. "He has to show us some fishing spots for the bigger fish."

Jack looked in the rearview mirror and caught Willy's gaze. "He'll be back out. He's just not staying with us."

Willy frowned.

Arriving at the police station, Jack parked the car. He, Cyrus, and the kids walked with Angela to the station from the parking lot.

A woman who looked like a grandma sat behind a counter.

She had short grey hair, glasses, bright red lips, and wore the same uniform as Angela. She was staring at the monitor in front of her and talking into the headset she wore. She smiled at Angela and signaled for Angela to wait. "Yes, Mrs. Martinson, there is a lot of traffic on Main Street. Mmm-hmm. Yes. I'll see if we can't have an officer in the area to make sure the good people of Pelican Rapids don't get run over crossing the street. Have a safe day." She ended the call and smiled at the group in the lobby.

"Good morning, Doris," Angela said.

"Good morning. You've brought some guests with you."

"Yes, this is Mr. Miller, and his kids Lynn and Willy."

"Good morning," Jack said. "Just call me Jack."

Angela shifted her gaze, "And this is mister?"

Cyrus interrupted her, stepped forward and reached over the counter. "I'm Cyrus." He gently shook Doris' hand, holding on until she pulled her hand away.

"It's nice to meet you all. I'm guessing you're all vacationing here since I don't know you."

Jack said, "The kids, my wife and I are staying in a cabin at the south end of South Lida. We'll be here a couple of weeks until the kids have to go back to school."

Cyrus added, "I've been here most of the summer. I'm staying out at the state park. I'm surprised I haven't seen you."

"Well, as long as you stay out of trouble, we probably won't see too much of each other," Doris said.

"Too bad I'm a nice guy," Cyrus said, and winked.

"Doris is our dispatcher," Angela said. "She knows everyone in town, probably the county. She's worked here a long time."

"Gives me a reason to get up every day," Doris added.

Angela stood between the kids, an arm around each of their shoulders and steered them to the desk. "The kids here have a mystery to solve. They need some access to our old dog license registrations."

"I love a mystery," Doris said. "What is it?"

Willy pulled the string necklace over his head and showed Doris the dog license.

She gently turned it over in her hand and read it through her glasses. "It's one of ours," she said. "Nineteen forty-two. That's about as old as me." She laughed.

"We found it in the lake at the state park swimming beach," Lynn said. "We want to see if we can find out who it belonged to."

Doris stood up from behind the desk. "Follow me back to the storage room. We've got some old boxes you can carefully go through. It's dusty, but I think you'll be able to find out who licensed the dog."

"I'm coming too," Cyrus said.

Doris led the kids and Cyrus down the hallway. Her voice trailed off. "My parents had a dog. Maybe it was theirs."

Jack refilled his coffee cup from the coffee station behind Doris' desk. "Thanks for that. This will make their day. Now, what mystery can I help you solve?"

"My office is back here," Angela said.

They started down the hallway. On the walls along the way there were awards, and some old black and white photos and some more current color photos. Jack stopped to look at them. In one of the photos, there was an old picture of a group of men in suit coats, white shirts open at the collar, standing in front of a store, Hokanson's Hardware.

Angela joined Jack. "The Hokansons have been around a while," she said. "They owned many of the first businesses here. There're rumors that they ran out anyone who tried to compete."

Jack moved down the hall and studied another. A parade picture with a convertible driving down Main Street. On the side of the car was a sign on the door, Mayor Hokanson. "I'm sensing a theme here," Jack said.

"Right, come on," Angela said. She led Jack to her office. They sat at a small conference table in the corner. "I'll just get right to it. Drugs have been getting worse in Otter Tail County and in Pelican Rapids. Last night wasn't the first OD we've had. But it's the first death. The whole recreational substance scene has been moving from alcohol to pot, to meth and it's moving to prescription drugs, opioids, heroin." Angela paused and looked up into Jack's eyes. "I need some help. It's getting worse. Fentanyl's getting mixed in and I'm afraid last night is the start of something bad."

"You've talked with the Sheriff's Department?" Jack asked.

Angela nodded. "I have, but they're not much help. I'm afraid they might be part of the problem."

"What do you mean?" Jack asked.

"Let me tell you about Pelican Rapids," Angela said. "We're a little town supporting summer tourism because we're close to so many lakes. We run on a few small businesses and a few big businesses. We've got the turkey plant, a log home building business, a regional delivery company, and a phone center. It's these big businesses that employ the majority of the people here. They provide regular hours, health benefits, a steady income."

"Sounds pretty good," Jack said.

"We're totally dependent on them. They're all run by one family, the Hokansons."

"And the Sheriff?"

"Hokansons get elected who they want. Who they can control."

"And you and your department?"

"We're hired, not elected. When an opening for an officer opened a couple of years ago, they recruited me. I worked under the previous chief. I think Hokanson had an influence; get a young female, someone they can control. The old chief retired and I got promoted."

Jack laughed. "And they got you, a headstrong, stubborn, tough female cop who is going to run the department the way it needs to be run."

Angela smirked. "You said it. I didn't. But, I still need to be careful how I handle the Hokansons. I want to keep the citizens safe and I want to keep my job. I need to be diplomatic."

Jack tipped back his coffee and finished it. "And why do you need me?"

"I'm stuck. I don't know who to trust. And I don't want another young person to OD on my streets. We have the Fall Music Festival, a huge country western concert, coming into the area in a couple of weeks. Lots of young people looking to party. The alcohol is bad enough. We'll have some DUI's and car accidents, some fights, but if these drugs are out there I fear we'll have some more deaths."

"I can offer up some ideas, but I'm on vacation. You want some true Fed help, I can call my boss in Minneapolis. But, I don't think it's a Fed issue right now."

"I just need someone to talk to, bounce some ideas off of. I'm starting to gather some evidence that's pointing to the Hokansons as the distributors, but I need more."

"Who can you trust?" Jack asked.

Angela ticked a list off on her fingers. "There's you, that's one. Doris is two, and I have an officer on my team, Dane Larby, and maybe another, that I trust completely. That's it on the enforcement side. There are a couple of families in town that I trust. I feel pretty alone against this. So many people here depend on the Hokansons for their jobs or they're afraid of them."

Jack sat and stared into the bottom of his coffee mug at

the few drops of liquid and some grounds. He thought about holding the high school girl last night while she shook, afraid as her friend was dying a few yards away. "Why don't you show me what you've got. I'll see if I can give you some ideas."

"Great," Angela said. She jumped up and headed to her desk. "I've got a few files over here I can walk you through."

Willy ran into the office. "Dad, we solved the mystery."

"That was quick," Jack said.

Lynn followed and put a white piece of paper on the table in front of Jack. "Here's a copy of the license application."

Cyrus stood in the door.

Willy grabbed the piece of paper and held it up for Jack to read and then jerked it back so he could read it himself. He pointed at the paper. "He was a male, named Sarge. The license cost fifty cents."

"He was licensed by Anton Hokanson in 1942," Lynn finished.

"Hokanson, huh? Isn't that interesting?" Jack turned his head and looked back at Cyrus. What did he know and what was behind the story he told last night by the fire? "Nice job, guys. I didn't think you'd solve it that fast."

Cyrus smirked, "Doris keeps good records and an orderly storage room."

Jack said to Angela, "That Hokanson name just keeps coming up."

Angela set her files on the table.

Jack asked Willy for the copy of the license and read it again. He thought about what Angela had said about her job, the drugs, and the Hokansons and about their run-in with Clint in the park, the street dance and the OD'd kids. Maybe it was time to meet the patriarch. "I think you, me and Cyrus should drive out to the Hokanson place and meet the old man. You need to give him an update on the drug issue and what you're doing about it. What's his name?"

"Otto," answered Angela. "What about reviewing my files?"

"We'll look at them later," Jack said. "Think the kids can hang with Doris if I buy lunch?"

"Sure," Angela said.

"I can stay with the kids," Cyrus said.

Jack shook his head. "No, I think you're coming with us. You and Clint have a history."

"Doris, can you call and let Mr. Hokanson know I'm coming out to see him?" Angela asked.

Jack answered. "Cancel that Doris. I think it's better if we just show up."

Doris smiled and looked at Angela for confirmation. Angela shrugged and nodded her agreement.

Jack handed Lynn thirty dollars. "You guys listen to Doris, learn how to run a police department and treat her to a nice lunch. We'll be back soon."

CHAPTER TWELVE

Angela drove, Cyrus sat in the front passenger seat. Jack sat in the middle of the backseat and leaned forward, his arms between the front bucket seats.

"Has Otto asked about what happened last night? Has he been concerned about the drugs?" Jack asked.

"No," Angela answered.

"If he's not involved, he should be concerned, right? He's the king of Otter Tail County or Pelican Rapids. He employs many of the people from around here. He has a huge festival coming up. He should be concerned and wonder what you're doing about it," Jack said. "I think it shows you're in front of this if you update him on what's going on. Let him know you have his concerns in mind and are trying to address them. And then maybe he won't think you suspect them of being behind it."

They turned left at the main stoplight in town and headed east.

"Where does he live?" Jack asked.

"They live on Lake Lida. The big lake north of the one

you're staying at. They have a large compound. It's impressive. It's just out past Stoney Bar."

"Stoney Bar?"

Angela chuckled. "You did just get here, didn't you." They drove past the hospital and swimming pool. "Stoney Bar is a piece of land, a bar, with a road that bisects the lakes; Lida and South Lida. There's a concrete box culvert connecting the two lakes so boats can go back and forth from one to the other. You'll use it when you get out fishing. Hokansons live out just past that on the north side of the road. Their house is right on the lake."

They drove on in silence for a bit and past the last house on the edge of town. Jack couldn't live here, too small. Angela asked, "Why are you two with me? What's the story behind that?"

"You're giving Cyrus a ride back out to his camper at the state park," Jack said.

"And you?" Angela asked. She caught his eye in the rearview mirror.

Jack hadn't thought this through. He'd just reacted, wanting to bring it to Otto Hokanson to see how he'd react.

"Tell him the truth," Cyrus said.

"Hey, he speaks," Jack laughed.

"The truth?" Angela asked.

Cyrus pulled a plastic-tipped cigar from his pocket. "Can I smoke?"

"As long as the window's down," Angela said. "What do you mean? The truth?"

After lighting the cigar and spitting out the window, Cyrus turned and said to Angela and Jack, "tell him the truth. Tell him Jack's an FBI agent in town on vacation. He was at the street dance last night and saw what happened and that he's offered to consult with you on the drug issue while he's here."

"Hmm, the truth." Jack thought about it. "I guess that works."

"OK," Angela said. "We have a plan."

THEY WOUND past a couple of farms on the two-lane county highway and drove past a golf course, an old resort and then followed the curve to the left by Maple Beach, a hamburger stand at an old resort. "You have to eat there," Cyrus said. "The best burgers and fries in the area. The kids will love it."

Jack frowned. The resort looked rough. A group of sagging cabins surrounded a main house and building. They all looked like they'd blow down in a heavy wind. Ripped screens covered the windows of the cabins. Cobwebs and dirt clung to the walls of the main building and under the eaves of all the buildings. The sign out front hadn't been painted in years. It was hard to read the name. People sat at about a dozen picnic tables in front of the main building, shaded by a few large trees.

Cyrus answered with a laugh. "It's better than it looks. It has a certain ambiance."

Angela added, "It's good."

Another quarter mile east, the two-lane road narrowed. Tight shoulders bounded the road and then the ground sloped down to large boulders and water on either side. Maybe about ten feet down. "This is Stoney Bar," Angela said. She pointed to the right. "Look out there, past the island, you can see the cabin you're staying at."

Jack thought he saw the cabin across the lake, past the island "How far is that?"

"A couple of miles?" Angela answered. "You can see South Lida is a lot smaller and looks quite different than Lida here on the left."

The lake on the left was big.

Jack watched as a fishing boat approached the road from South Lida. It disappeared, passing under them in the culvert Angela talked about. Jack turned and watched it slowly appear on the other side of the road. "I guess boats do fit through there," he said. The boat slowly accelerated and motored off onto Lida.

"Yep," Angela answered. "You just have to go through slowly, maybe raise the motor a bit. Depends on the water level."

On their right, as they reached the end of the bar, a boat launch parking lot was filled with trucks and trailers, the owners and boats all out on the lake for the day, fishing, skiing, and tubing or cruising.

Angela slowed and turned left between a couple of stone columns onto a blacktop driveway. Each column had a large metal script H affixed to it. "This is it."

The drive curved up between a row of maple trees and a manicured lawn. A large log house with a wraparound porch and a green, metal roof sat on top of a hill. "Nice place," Jack said.

Angela pulled the car around the circular drive and parked. "Otto, the dad, lives here with his son, Clint, who you met and he has a daughter, Hanna. One of their many businesses is a log home business."

They were doing OK, Jack thought. If business was good, why get into drug distribution? He answered his own question. He'd seen it before. Enough was never enough.

The log home had wide wooden stairs leading up to a porch that ran the length of it. In the center, double-doors with black, wrought-iron H's hanging on them, matching those on the pillars at the driveway entrance. Jack, Angela, and Clint exited the vehicle.

The double doors of the home opened and a tanned man with gray, slicked-back hair stepped out. Jack guessed he was in his fifties. He wore plaid shorts, a green polo shirt with a black H embroidered on the chest, Sperry deck shoes and a gold watch on his wrist. Sunglasses hid his eyes.

Jack watched as his expression changed. A smile appeared suddenly on his face. "Chief, welcome to my home. It's been a while."

"Mr. Hokanson, I've asked you to call me Angela." She led the trio up the steps, gently grasping Cyrus by the elbow to keep him steady as they climbed a few steps. Jack followed them up.

"Sorry we didn't call first. We were driving out to the state park and I decided to pull in. I wanted to talk with you about what happened last night at the street dance." Angela stepped forward, shook Otto's hand. "First, I'd like to introduce you to a couple of people." She stepped aside. "This is Cyrus."

Otto took Cyrus's hand and shook it. "Oh, we know each other."

"Really?" Angela asked. She turned her head, studied Cyrus' face and exchanged looks with Jack.

Cyrus kept a hold of Otto's hand. "Yep, we're related," Otto said.

"Distant cousins," Cyrus added.

Jack put a hand on Cyrus's shoulder and stepped forward to break the tension. He'd talk to Cyrus later about this new, surprising information. He held his hand out for a handshake.

Otto removed his hand from Cyrus' grasp and shook Jack's hand. "You must be Agent Miller with the FBI."

Jack hid his additional shock. Hokanson knew who he was. "You can call me Jack. I'm on vacation."

Otto held onto Jack's hand, gave it a squeeze, and then let go. He stepped aside. "Come on inside. I'll give you a short tour and we'll go back and sit on the deck facing the lake and talk."

Jack trailed behind the group, following Otto through the

house. He studied the furnishing and the walls. He'd learned that you could tell a lot about a person by what he surrounded himself with. The furniture was big and comfortable. In Otto's office the wall hangings were paintings, originals, he guessed, of outdoor scenes. Family photos appeared to be in frames on some of the shelves. Jack walked behind the massive oak desk to examine the photos on the wall. Some were old, 1920s or 30s.

Otto joined Jack to look at the photos. "A reminder of where it started; logging, transportation, and shipping..."

"And bootlegging it appears," Jack added.

Otto laughed. "Yes, the family made some benefits from prohibition. You'll see the sentiment of prohibition hung on. Otter Tail County used to be a dry county and Pelican Rapids was a dry town for years. Now we have a municipal liquor store, alcohol served in some of the restaurants." They stared at the pictures together. Otto continued, "And the Hokanson family built on the foundation of our original businesses." He looked around the room. "This home is one example of a premier home we produce, sell and construct. And we've added onto our portfolio of businesses over the years. In addition to transportation, we have real-estate, construction, phone centers, and some light manufacturing and food processing. Thinking about opening a brewpub in town. We're proud of the support that the Hokanson family can provide the lake area families with jobs."

"That's quite the legacy to leave," Jack replied. He picked up a picture from the desk. It was a picture of Otto standing on the steps to the house, framed by a young man and woman. "Your kids? Leaving it to these two?"

Otto took the photo from Jack, smiled, and pointed at the image. "The three. That's my son, Clint. I heard you met in town."

Jack smiled. "That's one way of putting it."

"Regrettable," Otto answered. "And the girl is my daughter, Hanna. She's pregnant, so I have a legacy of three."

"Congratulations. You're going to be a grandfather. That will be nice," Jack said.

"Thank you," Otto responded. He placed the photo back on its spot on his desk. Tweaking it until he had it right where he wanted it. "Well, enough about me and the Hokansons. Why don't we move out to the deck and get down to the incident from last night."

Outside, the four of them sat down at the table looking out over the lake.

"I forget what a beautiful view you have here, Mr. Hokanson," Angela said.

"I don't get tired of it. It's different every day."

A high school aged girl, wearing a uniform of shorts and shirt, brought out a pitcher of lemonade and glasses for them at the table. "Thank you, Kate," Otto said. She poured them each a glass and returned to the house.

"Do you get to enjoy the lake?" Jack asked.

"Not much more than the view. Once in a while I'll get out to fish."

"Cyrus was giving my kids some fishing tips on the dock this morning. I'm hoping we can use what he's taught us and enjoy the fishing over the next couple of weeks," Jack said.

"You're on the lake?" Otto asked.

"We're in a cabin on South Lida."

Otto nodded. "It's a nice little lake. Right, Cyrus? A little quieter and some good fishing."

Cyrus took a drink of lemonade. "Used to be, back in the day. We'll see if we can find them some fishing spots to try."

They all sat in silence and took a drink of lemonade.

"So, Angela. What do we know about the drugs and the overdoses last night?"

"Two victims. Both Pelican Rapids high school students. One is doing better. We had one fatality."

"It's just terrible what these drugs have done to our community and the young people," Otto said.

"When the survivor feels a little stronger, I'll be questioning them on where they got the drugs. See if we can't narrow in on the suppliers and get rid of them."

"And Agent Miller, your involvement?" Otto asked.

"I'm on vacation."

Angela jumped in. "I've asked him to give me a little of his time to take a look at this from an outsiders viewpoint. I feel terrible interrupting his vacation, but he's been gracious and said yes. I know what drugs would do to your workforce if the problem got too bad. And with the Festival coming up, I wanted to get ahead of this."

"Thank you, I appreciate that," Otto said. "And Cyrus, what's your involvement?"

Cyrus coughed and took a drink of lemonade. "The Miller's were kind enough to put me up last night and I'm just tagging along today. Angela's giving me a ride out to the state park to my camper when we're done here."

"I heard you were in town, but I feel bad we haven't connected. You could've stayed here. We have plenty of room. How long are you going to be around?"

"I'm good. I like it out at the state park and I hate to impose on anyone. I'm ready to get back to my camper, fish a little, maybe show Jack's kids how to fish and relax." Cyrus started coughing. Angela handed him his glass. After a drink, he continued. "I've been around for a while. Catching up with the area after being gone for so long. I'll be gone before long. I think I've found what I was looking for with homecoming."

Otto stared at Cyrus and then turned his attention back to Angela. "Is there anything I can do to help you?"

"No, I just wanted to stop by and give you a quick update.

Let you know I'm on top of it and that I was getting some assistance from Agent Miller." Angela pushed back from the table and stood up. "We've taken up enough of your time."

Jack stood up and signaled to Cyrus to stay seated. "I think Cyrus could use a little more lemonade to get his cough under control. Mind if I take a walk down to the lake and take a look? It looks so nice and I doubt I'll be back here to enjoy the view some other time."

Otto stood up as well. "I'll have Kate bring out fresh drinks and join you at the lake."

It was about fifty yards from the deck to the shore of the lake. Jack walked across the lush lawn, his feet slowly sinking into the grass with each step. At the lake there was a fire pit with a brick patio around it, surrounded by Adirondack chairs. A screened cabana sat off to the side. The grass was trimmed right up to the rocky shore. A dock, six feet wide, reached out from the shore. At the end, it branched off to the right with dock berths for a pontoon, a combo fishing-ski boat and a couple of jet skis. Jack walked out to the end of the dock and looked out over the lake.

"What do you think, Agent Miller?" Otto walked out onto the dock to join him, puffing on a cigar.

"Call me Jack. I'm on vacation."

"You can call me Otto."

"I feel like I'm at a resort. The house is beautiful, the lawn is flawless and this beach area is great." He turned toward the boats. "And look at these. A different boat for every need."

"Well, I'm a lucky man," Otto replied. "None of this is my doing, directly." He waved the cigar in the air. "But it's the result of working hard. I hire for the roles I need. It gives me the time to focus. I always say, do what you're best at."

"A family legacy," Jack said.

"Much of this land along the lake and back to the road and to the east was farmland that my family started with long ago. They worked hard. I try to work hard but smarter. Less physical."

"Well, you've done well. And it's nice to have this view to retreat to before and after a hard day."

Otto puffed on the cigar again and exhaled into the air. "It is."

CHAPTER THIRTEEN

B ack on the deck, Jack and Otto joined Angela, Cyrus, and another woman. The woman was very pregnant, ready to give birth any day now based on what Jack remembered about Julie and her pregnancies. Jack was glad he didn't see Clint on the deck. He didn't need that headache now.

Angela introduced him to Hanna.

"It's nice to meet you," Jack said. "And congratulations. I probably shouldn't say this, but it looks like you're close?"

"Thanks," Hanna responded. "Due in a few weeks. I'm glad the timing worked out for after the Festival."

Otto put his arm around Hanna and hugged her. "Yes, the timing is good, the pregnancy is going great and we're all excited to see who is joining the family."

Jack caught Angela's eye and nodded towards the front door. It was time to go.

Angela said, "Mr. Hokanson, thank you for your hospitality this morning. I just wanted to update you on last night and let you know we're working on putting an end to the drug problem in town and in the county."

"You didn't have to come all the way out here, but I appreciate it. I have every confidence that you'll get ahead of this, and it's good to see you have the help of the FBI." He turned to Jack. "But please, enjoy your vacation. I'm sure you didn't come here to work."

"Thanks, I think the Chief here knows what she's doing." Jack grabbed Cyrus by the elbow and pointed him towards the front door. "But I'll help how I can."

ANGELA DROVE DOWN THE DRIVEWAY. "Let's go get Cyrus his meds while we're here," Jack said. "Then we can go back to town and bring him to his truck."

Angela turned left onto the county highway, heading to the state park. Jack leaned forward between the seats. "What the heck, Cyrus, you're related to those guys?"

Cyrus pulled a box of Swisher Sweets out of his pocket. "May I?" he asked Angela.

Angela pushed the buttons on her armrest and lowered the windows. "Go ahead."

Cyrus spit out the window, pulled a cigar out of the box and lit it. After a couple of puffs and exhales out the window, he turned in his seat to face Jack and Angela. He hung his right arm, holding the cigar, out the window. "We're cousins, kind of. My mom and Otto's grandfather were siblings."

"Kind of cousins?" Jack thought about it. "So, Otto's mom or dad is your cousin?"

"Was."

"OK, *was* your cousin. So, what was that in the park with you and Clint? A family squabble between second or third cousins?" Jack asked.

"Clint's my cousin, twice removed." Cyrus turned away, took another puff from his cigar and blew the smoke out the window.

"That would have been nice to know before we went out there, don't you think?" Jack asked.

Cyrus kind of shrugged, but didn't say anything.

Jack sat back in his seat. "Now, that we've got the family tree down, what was the fight about? You and Clint and Otto don't seem to be kissing cousins." Jack said.

Angela chuckled and Cyrus smiled.

The car slowed and Angela turned right into the state park. A paved two-lane road wound through rolling hills and prairie grasslands.

Cyrus took another puff from his cigar and then a coughing fit started.

"Ever think you should quit smoking?" Angela asked.

After getting his hacks under control, Cyrus spoke. "I'm too old to try and quit. I like it." He twisted in his seat and spoke to Jack. "I grew up here, but I've been gone a long time. Once I entered the Navy, I never came back, except for my mom's funeral. Now I'm back, I've been asking around trying to get some old questions answered. Guess Clint didn't like it. He wants me to leave and go back to Chicago."

"Questions?" Jack asked.

"Just old family stuff."

"How long are you going to be around?" Angela asked.

Cyrus smiled and took a long drag from his cigar. "Not too much longer."

"You're not going to tell us any more?" Jack asked.

"It's just family stuff. Not important," Cyrus answered.

"This is the first you've talked to Otto all summer?" Jack asked.

"I've been lucky not to run into him," Cyrus replied. "But I don't know how much he gets out." Cyrus took another puff. "But he knows I'm here. Clint's seen me, knows who I am and I'm sure reported on our encounters."

Jack thought Cyrus had more to say but didn't believe he was in a place to share it yet.

"And he knew I was FBI," Jack said. He caught Angela's eye in the rearview mirror.

"I didn't tell him," she said.

"Well, someone did, or he's researched me with my arrival. The people that own the cabin we're staying in?" Jack shook his head. "I don't know. Probably not important. I just have to assume he knows more about me than we've said." He sat back in his seat. "Let's go find Cyrus' camper, get his meds and get back into town before my kids take over the police station."

Angela slowed to a stop at the park ranger building and waved. The ranger waved her through. Following the road through the park, Cyrus directed Angela to the campground. "It's that pop-up over there." The camper sat on a gravel pad under a couple of trees. The ends were extended out. The flaps were up on the windows and the door was closed. A small grill sat by a picnic table not far from the camper, along with an old folding chair.

Jack got out of the car, followed by Cyrus. Angela stayed in the car and checked her phone.

"Is it comfortable?" Jack asked.

"It's enough for me," Cyrus said. "As long as it keeps the mosquitos out, I'm good. I sleep well. It's almost like being outside when you open all the window flaps."

"Looks like you've had it for a while," Jack said.

"She's not pretty, but she holds a lot of memories. My wife and I did a lot of traveling and camping together around lake Michigan and the Upper Peninsula."

Jack studied Cyrus and thought about him pulling the camper around Michigan, sitting at picnic tables with his wife, laughing, playing cards. "You never brought her here?"

Cyrus didn't meet Jack's gaze. "No, maybe I should have,

it's a beautiful place, especially this time of year. She would've liked this."

Jack let Cyrus have some time with his thoughts. Angela caught his eye and pointed at her wrist to hurry them along. "Well, get your meds, maybe open it up a little to get some fresh air in there and we'll get back to town for lunch and your truck."

Cyrus opened the door and started to step in. "Dang it," he said. He stopped and backed out. "Come here, Jack," Cyrus said.

Jack stepped over to Cyrus.

"Look inside. Somebody's ransacked my camper." Cyrus' shoulders slumped and he shook his head.

Jack stuck his head in the camper. Cushions were ripped open, food, pots and pans were all over the place inside. Clothes lay in piles on the floor and on the small counter by the stove. "Who'd you piss off?"

"Just Clint."

"Where are your meds?" Jack asked.

"There's a drawer on the other side of the stove."

Jack waved for Angela to get her attention and signaled her to come over and join them. "Why don't you sit at the picnic table. We'll ask Angela how to handle this and then I'll grab your meds."

Angela stood at the end of the table. "What's up?" she asked.

Jack led Angela over to the camper. "Somebody vandalized Cyrus' camper."

"What?" Angela stuck her head in the camper. "Who could've done this?"

Jack frowned. "I think we all know who the primary suspect is. Who do we call? The Park Rangers? You're the police and already here."

"I think the sheriff would handle this. I'll call the ranger station."

"OK, I'm going to grab his meds and then when you're all ready, we can get back to town."

"Cyrus can't stay here tonight," Angela said.

"No, I'll call Julie and let her know we have a guest again tonight. We'll just leave his truck in town where it is."

WHILE THE PARK Ranger and Angela sat at the table talking with Cyrus, Jack called the Pelican Rapids police station and talked with Doris and asked her to let his kids know they'd be back soon. Then he called Julie and updated her on what happened at the camper and that Cyrus would be spending another few nights with them. He couldn't let him stay here and they had to keep an eye on him while Clint was on the prowl.

This might give him a chance to learn more about the Hokansons and what Cyrus wasn't sharing.

CHAPTER FOURTEEN

"Kate!" Otto bellowed. "Bring me a drink. Something strong." He sat with Hanna on the patio. "What was that about? The three of them out here?"

"Could it be as simple as Angela was taking Cyrus back to his camper?" Hanna asked.

Otto snorted. "No. There's something going on. Angela stops in with Cyrus and the FBI agent?"

Kate delivered his drink. Otto swallowed it in one shot. "Where's your brother?" Otto felt his arms quivering. He wasn't sure what it was. Anger? It couldn't be fear. Could it? The Festival was less than a week away and now this: overdoses, a visit by the FBI. "Where is he?"

"I think he's gaming," Hanna said.

"Kate! Get that son of mine and tell him to get his ass out here. It's time for lunch."

Otto looked across the table at Hanna. "What happens if we don't go forward with this drug business at the festival?"

"We don't hit our numbers for our projections. A few of our businesses are weak and behind on earnings. We can still use the festival for laundering some money and it will make us some cash. But we have this one opportunity this year to launder the drug money. It comes in later and we'll have to sit on it until next year's festival."

Otto sat back in his chair. He wasn't ready to give up yet. He smiled at Hanna. "You feeling OK? You look a little off, pale or something."

Hanna pointed at her plate. "Toast was all I could think about eating this morning. I'm ready to get this thing out of me."

Clint shuffled onto the deck in a t-shirt and basketball shorts. His hair was a mess. He plopped down into the chair between Hanna and Otto.

"Good afternoon," Otto said.

Clint nodded and lit a cigarette.

"You missed some visitors this morning. Chief Angela, Cyrus and FBI Agent Miller were here."

"What'd they want?" Clint asked.

"That's what Hanna and I were just talking about," Otto said. "I don't know why they were here. Angela said it was to update me on the overdoses at the street dance." He paused. "And to show me she had the FBI helping her, I guess. But, I don't believe it."

"OK," Clint said.

Otto thought Clint looked a little guilty. "You look like you've got something on your mind," Otto said. "What is it?"

"I just thought they might have been out here asking about Cyrus' camper."

"Why?" Otto asked.

Clint looked away and answered, "I went out and searched it after my run in with him at the park in Pelican."

"Searched it for what?"

"I want to find the gold. I was looking for maps, notes, the gold itself."

"Clint, what are you doing?" Otto asked. "The Festival is

coming up and everything depends on that. Nothing else. Forget the gold." Otto waited for Clint to look at him. "Got it?"

Clint nodded. "I go it."

"OK," Otto said. "I do have something else for you. I need you to find out about this agent: where he's staying, when they're there, what they're driving. All that info."

"I got it," Clint said. "I'll see what I can find."

Otto got up from the table. "Take care of yourself," he said to Hanna. To Clint, he said, "I trust you can get this done." Then he went inside to his office. He had some phone calls to make.

CHAPTER FIFTEEN

"OK. Everybody ready? Sunscreen, life jackets, bait, water, snacks?" Julie asked.

Vince waded through the shallow water along the shore searching for frogs, fish or whatever caught a dog's attention while the kids stood on the grass at the end of the dock, fishing poles in hand.

"Yes, we're ready," Lynn answered.

"Can we please go fishing now?" Willy pleaded.

Jack helped Cyrus step down into the boat from the dock. "We're just going fishing for a couple of hours, right?" Jack asked. He laughed. "It looks like we're setting off on an expedition."

"Do you have the boat keys and the fishing license?" Julie asked.

Jack tapped his pockets, making sure he had them. "Got 'em. Let's load up the boat and go catch some fish."

"Yeah!" the kids yelled and took off towards the boat, fishing poles in hand.

"Don't run on the dock!" Julie yelled after them. She grabbed her fishing pole and picked up the cooler by the handle and followed them. "Come on, Vince. You're going too." Vince jumped onto the shore, shook himself off and ran down the dock after the kids.

After helping everybody get in the boat and settled in seats, Jack backed the boat away from the dock and then slowly drove out onto the lake. Cyrus sat in the seat to his left, Julie behind him and the kids in the open bow in the front, with Vince between them. "There were some notes in the cabin binder on where to fish. Have any spots we should check out Cyrus?"

"Let's cruise the lake and I'll point out some spots. Then we can go over to the big lake and I'll point out some others and we can pick one or two to try." He pointed to the bay to the east. "Let's go over there first."

Jack pushed forward on the throttle. He wore his baseball cap backward to keep it from blowing off his head. He adjusted his sunglasses and smiled. This felt like the vacation he'd planned. The bow of the 19-foot Lund boat lifted up out of the water as the 150-horsepower motor pushed them forward. The boat planed out and rushed over the water. The kids cheered and raised their arms in the air. They entered the bay and Cyrus pointed to a reed bed on the east end. Jack slowed the boat as the neared it.

"Any time of day or sunny afternoons like this, if you anchor in close to the reeds, you should be able to catch some Crappies. Mornings or after supper, troll the edge or along that north shore, cast and retrieve and you might find some Crappies or Walleye, maybe a Northern Pike." Cyrus pointed at the depth finder screen attached to the dash of the boat. "Use that, to see the depth of the water. Try different depths and if you find the fish, you know better where they're hanging out, what depth to fish."

"Can we fish now?" Willy asked.

Jack answered, "We're going to tour the lake. Listen to

Cyrus' recommendations so we know what to do when he's not around. We'll be fishing soon."

"Let's cruise around the island, head over to the big lake and we'll find a couple of spots there to try this afternoon. I'm hungry for fish," Cyrus said.

Jack accelerated and followed Cyrus' directions on where to go to avoid rocks and sandbars and where to try to find fish later. The breeze felt good with the speed of the boat, cooling them off from the afternoon sun. After about a mile or so, they were approaching the north end of the lake and the culvert that connected the two lakes. Cyrus motioned with his hand for Jack to slow the boat.

"Aim for the culvert opening if nobody is coming through from the other side," Cyrus said. He pointed at the throttle handle. "Use the button there to raise the motor a little to make sure the propeller doesn't hit the bottom."

Jack pushed the button and the motor tilted up a little. He steered them for the opening a little faster than idle speed. The boat slipped through the opening. It felt cooler as soon as they got in the shadow of the tunnel.

"Look at all the writing," Lynn said. Her voice echoed a little in the culvert.

The concrete walls of the culvert were covered in graffiti, spray-painted names in many different colors. They slowly drove through, coming out the other side. The lake in front of them looked a lot bigger than the lake they came from. It was more circular and further across.

About twenty yards out of the culvert, Cyrus told Jack it was OK to lower the motor and give it some gas. He pointed out a couple of other weed beds that would be good for bass or sunfish.

Jack sped to the east and then slowed the boat about fifty yards from shore.

"Wow, look at that place," Lynn said.

"That's the Hokanson's home," Jack said.

"It's beautiful," Julie said.

The green lawn ran up from the lake to the log home. The gardens of bushes and flowers framed the picture, drawing the eye. It looked even better from the lake than it had close up. "It's a nice place, inside and out," Jack said. "And it's a beautiful view of the lake from their deck." He took his cell phone out and took a few pictures. "How's the fishing here, Cyrus?"

"We can check it out. Can you kids drop the anchor in the lake?" Cyrus asked.

"Sure," Willy said.

"Be careful with the rope so you don't get tangled in it," Cyrus added.

Willy and Lynn lifted the anchor together and dropped it into the lake and watched it sink to the bottom. Cyrus showed them how to tie off the rope on the cleat.

"Jack, what are you doing stopping here?" Julie asked in a quiet voice.

Jack turned his ball cap around the right way, the bill shading his face. The gold embroidered letters FBI stood out on the navy blue front panel of the cap. He took off his sunglasses, winked at her and smiled. "We're fishing."

OTTO STOOD on his deck and shielded his eyes with his hand to block the sun. "Who's sitting out there?" The lake was open access, but most people knew that the area in front of the Hokanson's was off-limits for a couple of hundred yards. They didn't want people sitting out in front of their home wrecking their view, blocking access to the lake.

There was a boat full of people closer to shore. "Grab the binoculars for me," he said to Clint.

Clint returned with the binoculars. "You want me to go run them off?"

"Just wait." Otto raised the binoculars to his eyes and brought the boat into focus. The green Lund fishing boat was anchored. He saw the rope stretched out from the front of the boat. "They've got the whole family out there fishing."

"Who?" Clint asked.

His grip tightened while he continued to focus on the boat. "It's our friend, Special Agent Miller. He's got the whole family out there fishing. His wife, son, and daughter, his dog," he paused, "and Cyrus." Otto handed the binoculars to Clint.

"I can get them to leave."

"No," Otto said. "We'll let it go. This time." Otto sat at the table. "We'll keep an eye on them here. Sit down."

Clint pulled up a chair and watched the boat. "Looks like they caught something."

"Put the glasses down." Otto waited to get Clint's attention. "Look at me, Clint. I want to make sure you're paying attention."

Clint set the binoculars on the table.

"Look at me. Listen to my words." Otto said.

"I'm listening."

Otto stared into Clint's eyes to make sure he had his attention. "The festival is in five days. We can't have anything interfere with that."

Otto picked up the binoculars and focused in on the boat again. "I need to get you a new hat, Agent Miller." He glanced at Clint. "Are you still here? Go find Angela and talk to her while we know these guys are out on the lake."

CHAPTER SIXTEEN

Jack added some more wood to the campfire. The kids were playing corn hole against Cyrus and Julie. Jack couldn't tell if the kids were just better at tossing the beanbags or if Cyrus and Julie were giving them a break, but the kids were ahead.

The sun dipped lower on the horizon and the mosquitoes started to come out. Jack grabbed the mosquito spray and doused his arms, legs, and neck and settled into one of the Adirondack chairs by the fire.

The kids cheered and ran over to the fire. "We won, dad!" Willy said.

"High fives!" Jack held out his palms to exchange slaps with the kids. Julie walked with Cyrus as he limped over to the fire circle to join them. "Here come the losers," Jack said.

"Hey, that's harsh." Julie helped Cyrus into a chair. "They're pretty good," she said. "It wasn't even close."

"I didn't help much," Cyrus added. "I need to practice and then we'll have a rematch."

Jack handed Cyrus a beer. "To drown your sorrows."

They all sat in a circle and watched the fire burn. It

crackled and snapped and the red coals glowed in the darkening night. "This was a good day," Jack said. "Why don't we go around and say what we liked about it." After a pause, he continued. "I'll start. I thought the fish dinner tonight was excellent. Thanks for putting us on some great fishing holes and showing us how to fry the fish, Cyrus."

Cyrus raised his beer to Jack and they clinked bottles in a toast.

"I'll go next," Willy said. He held up the dog tag hanging from the fishing line. "We solved the case of the old dog tag today."

"Great detective work by you guys," Julie said. "Lynn, you next?"

Jack took a sip of his beer and thought about the tie-in to Hokansons from so long ago. A coincidence that they found the dog tag where Julie lost her ring? The dog tag belonged to one of the Hokansons relative's dogs? And that Cyrus had a story putting it there?

Lynn stood. "I caught my first fish today and it was the biggest."

"That was an excellent battle," Cyrus said.

"And we learned how to clean a fish," Willy added.

"And did it well," Cyrus said.

Jack chimed in, "I didn't catch any fish."

"Somebody had to drive the boat," Julie said.

"We'll still let you eat, Dad," Lynn said. She sat down. "Your turn, Mom."

Julie started to talk. "I'm just glad..."

Jack's phone buzzed, interrupting her. He dug it out of his pocket, checked the screen and stood. "Sorry, I have to get this. I'll be right back."

"We'll be right back," Julie said, and followed him. "I'll get the stuff for s'mores."

"This is Jack. What's up?" Jack said into the phone as he

walked to the cabin.

Julie tapped him on the shoulder. He turned. "Who is it?" she mouthed.

"Just a sec," he said into the phone. "It's Agent Kiley," he said to Julie. Then he returned to the call. "OK, what's up?" He walked into the cabin. Julie followed and the screen door slammed shut behind her.

Jack sat at the table and had a conversation with Agent Kiley. When he was done, Julie was standing, leaning against the kitchen island, her arms crossed.

"I thought we were on vacation," Julie said.

"We are," Jack answered. "Today was a great day." He walked over and stood in front of Julie. "This has been the first call."

"Did you call the headhunter back today?"

Jack shook his head. "I forgot."

"Forgot?"

Jack grabbed Julie's hands and held them in his. They were warm and soft. "I'll call her back tomorrow."

"What did Agent Kiley need?"

"They think tonight's Amtrak might have a drug shipment on it. They didn't find anything in St. Paul, but they want me to stake out a couple of the stops along the way tonight since I'm up this way."

Julie lowered her head and shook it back and forth a couple of times.

"The stops are up this way. It stops in Staples at one twenty-six in the morning. You all go to sleep. I'll have a late night."

She looked into his eyes and frowned. "We're on vacation."

"I'm just staking it out. No engagement." Jack stepped forward and wrapped his arms around Julie. "I'm sorry."

Julie took a deep breath and blew it out into his chest. "Be careful. And call the headhunter tomorrow."

"I promise."

She wiggled out of his hug and grabbed the tray of supplies. "Let's go make some s'mores."

BACK AT THE FIRE, Julie handed out the roasting sticks and marshmallows.

"I didn't get to say what I was thankful for yet," Cyrus said. The firelight sparkled in his eyes. "I just want you all to know how thankful I am that you've all taken me in these past couple of days." He smiled and swiped a finger at the corner of his eye. Then he started coughing.

"We're happy you could spend this time with us," Julie said. Everybody agreed.

Lynn handed him a s'more she made. "Do you have another story for us?" she asked.

Cyrus stared up at the sky, tracing the path of embers from the fire up into the air. "I have one I think you'll enjoy, but my throats a little scratchy."

"Kids, can you please go get us all something to drink?" Julie asked. "Then story time will begin."

The kids ran off to get the drinks. Julie asked Cyrus, "Are you doing OK?"

"I'm doing great. Thanks."

"Really?" Julie asked.

Cyrus reached out for Julie's hand and held it. "Really. I loved spending the day with you all. I can't thank you enough for letting me hang out with you all and taking care of me."

Julie smiled. "It's been our pleasure," she said.

The kids returned and passed out the beverages. Everyone settled into their seats and opened their drinks. Jack put some more wood on the fire. The sun had set further and the yellows in the sky had disappeared. A lone loon called out on the lake.

Willy and Lynn sat at Cyrus' feet and got ready to listen.

Cyrus cleared his throat, took a drink and started.

"This is a story that my mother told me. A family tale." He paused, smiled and started the story. "The Civil War between the North and the South took place in the 1860s. My great-great-great grandpa, Harold Jacobson, fought for the North as part of the Scandinavian Regiment out of Minnesota and Wisconsin, made up of Norwegians and Swedes. He made it through the war and came back to Minnesota. And he brought some things home with him. He had his musket, uniform, some other weapons and," Cyrus paused before continuing.

"And what?" Willy asked.

"And a bag of Confederate gold dollars."

Willy and Lynn looked at each other. "Where are they?" asked Lynn.

Cyrus stopped for a drink, cleared his throat and continued.

"He used a little of the gold to buy some land here in Otter Tail County."

Lynn interrupted, "Wait. Where'd the gold come from?"

"Towards the end of the war, the Confederates were shipping gold out of cities before they fell to the North. The Scandinavian Regiment intercepted one of the shipments and decided to split it up among themselves and let the rebels go free."

"How much did he get?" Willy asked.

"That's part of the mystery," Cyrus answered. "We don't really know. We do know he used a little of his share of the gold to buy some land here, but the story is that he had a lot left. He didn't want to splurge and make it known that he had all this gold. And Scandinavians aren't known for splurging. And he may have felt a little guilty for taking it. He just wanted his own farm and to start a family. And kept the gold for emergencies."

"Where is it?" Lynn asked.

Cyrus smiled. His eyes twinkling from the reflected flames and his teeth showing their whiteness against the dark of the night. "That's what I'm trying to find out."

"You have your own mystery," Willy said.

"Yep, and it's tied to the other story I told you the other night."

"How?" Julie jumped in.

A laugh erupted from Cyrus, followed by a coughing fit. He held up his hand to show he was all right. When he got his cough under control, he answered. "The man running from the dogs and men in the last story was running because he found the gold hidden at the farm. He got away with a bag of gold coins and the treasure was never seen again."

"You're looking for it, aren't you?" Julie asked.

"It's a family story that's been around for a long time. Nobody knows if it's true, but I figured now was a good time to look for it."

Jack finally asked a question. "Is this the reason for your run-in with Clint and Otto?"

"It's probably part of it," Cyrus answered. "I don't want them to have the money and I'd hate for it to disappear when I'm gone. They've heard some of the same stories I have and I'm sure Otto would love to have the gold."

"That's why you have the metal detector," Julie said.

Cyrus nodded. "I've looked around the parkland. The original farm was back there before it was a park."

"That's why you're camping there?" Lynn asked.

"One of the reasons," Cyrus said. "I figured that if the

story is true about him running, he must've dumped the gold somewhere between the farm and the lake. He couldn't swim from the island to the western shore carrying a heavy bag of gold. He'd sink."

"Wow," Willy whispered. "Your own treasure mystery."

"It's our secret," Cyrus said.

Jack stared at Cyrus and thought back through the two stories; the man running and fighting with the dog and his great, great grandfather having the gold. There were connections and pieces missing. Things he believed Cyrus knew, but wasn't sharing. He considered bringing it up now, but decided to wait until the kids went to bed. "That's quite the story, Cyrus. Now, I think it's time for the kids to go to bed."

"Dad, not yet," Lynn pleaded.

"Yep, now. We'll hear more from Cyrus later. Now, let's go get ready for bed." Jack helped the kids up from their chairs. He turned to Julie and Cyrus, "Can I bring you another beer when I return?" They both nodded.

JACK JOINED Julie and Cyrus at the fire and handed out the cold bottles of beer. "You're full of surprises, aren't you, Cyrus?"

"I can't afford to keep too many secrets much longer. Or they'll die with me. What do you want to know?"

Jack closed his eyes while he tried to form his assumptions and the questions he wanted answered. He took a long pull off the bottle, swallowed, quietly belched and then started. "Your mother told you these stories. You're related to the Hokansons. The man who took the gold and ran. He was your father?"

Cyrus nodded. "You are a trained FBI agent, aren't you?

My mother was Otto's great-aunt. She was Otto's grandfather's sister. Otto's father was my cousin. The man who took the gold was my father. He and my mother were seeing each other, but not married. But after that confrontation, she thought they'd kill him. He fled, joined the army and was killed in the war, World War Two. I never met him. I was raised by my mother. She was kind of ostracized from the family. Out of the family because she got pregnant out of wedlock and because her boyfriend stole the family gold. It was rough growing up. She stayed but wanted me to leave for my own good. As soon as I was old enough, I enlisted in the Navy. Never came back except for her funeral. She died of cancer while I was in Vietnam."

"I'm so sorry," Julie said.

Cyrus waved it away. "It's nothing. I had a great wife, a good life. But, it's almost over."

"Is there really gold?" Jack asked.

"I think there is," Cyrus answered. "I don't know how much, but I think it's a lot based on some of the things my mother told me. I think she knew where it was, but left it hidden to punish her family for the way they treated her, and me. One reason Otto is so concerned with my showing up here this summer is I might know where the gold is."

Jack thought back over the last few days. Pieces were starting to fit together. "That's why your camper was ransacked?"

Cyrus shrugged. "Maybe."

"Anything else you want to share?" Jack asked.

"No, nothing I can think of. I would like to find the gold."

"What would you do with it?" Julie asked.

Cyrus stared into the fire as he answered. "I've thought about that. I want to find it to spite the Hokansons more than anything else, but I'd like to gift it to the town of Pelican

Rapids, in memory of my mother. But, I need to figure out how to keep it in control of the people and not Otto and his family."

"If you find it," Julie said.

"When I find it," Cyrus answered.

CHAPTER SEVENTEEN

"Coffee now?" Cyrus asked. "You'll be able to sleep?"

Jack sat down at the table on the screened-in porch with Julie and Cyrus and set his steaming mug down. They'd moved inside to get away from the bugs. Moths and mosquitoes covered the outside of the screens, attracted to the lights on the porch. "I have to go out for a while," Jack said.

Cyrus checked his watch. "Where you off to this late?"

"That's what I said. I told him we're on vacation," Julie said.

"I got a call from an agent in Minneapolis. She wants me to check a couple of Amtrak stations when the train comes through tonight."

"When you leaving? Want some company?" Cyrus asked. "I don't sleep much anymore."

Jack pulled out his phone, checked the time and opened Google maps. The directions said the drive was an hour and fifteen minutes. "The train gets to Staples at one twenty-six. I don't know how Amtrak does on the schedule up here, but I know they left St. Paul on time. I'm going to finish my coffee and leave." He slipped his phone back in his pocket. "That'll put me at the Staple Amtrak station about thirty minutes before the train gets there. You're free to come with me." Jack would normally go alone, but this was just sitting in the car, watching the train. He doubted he'd even see anything. Kiley wasn't positive anything was coming through. With some time in the car, he and Cyrus could talk and clear up a few things that were still bothering him about Cyrus, his stories and the Hokansons.

Cyrus pushed himself up from the table. "Let me hit the head and grab some coffee for the road."

Jack emptied his coffee mug and leaned over to Julie. He kissed her cheek. "Get some sleep."

Julie didn't look at him, but nodded her head. She reached over and squeezed his leg. "I love you. Be careful."

"Talking with Cyrus will help me stay awake. Tell him to meet me out at the car." Jack left and quietly shut the screen door.

JACK TURNED LEFT from the gravel road onto the paved county highway and headed south. The sky was black and clear, filled with sparkling stars. "It's going to take me a few more nights to get used to all the stars you can see here," Jack said.

"It is pretty amazing," Cyrus answered. "We could barely see Venus in Chicago with all the city lights. You forget what a night sky looks like." After a pause, he asked, "You know where you're going?"

"I got it routed on Google Maps. We have some time, so I'm taking the back roads." He pushed the button starting the route in the app.

"Just watch out for deer. There isn't an app for that yet."

Jack laughed. "Thanks, now everything will look like a deer."

Cyrus pulled a cigar out of his pocket. "Mind if I smoke?"

"I'll crack the windows." Jack lowered the front and back windows down a little bit. "Have another one? I'll join you."

Cyrus lit the first cigar and handed it to Jack. Then he lit another for himself. He blew the smoke out the window. "You know, Jack. You've got a great family."

"Thanks." Jack stared out the window and thought about how good it felt to have them all together for a vacation. He felt a little guilty going out on this assignment tonight. "I'm glad we could do this vacation. Julie and I were apart for a few months but we got back together after the Fourth of July."

"What happened?" Cyrus asked. "I mean if you want to talk about it."

"Julie likes the Twin Cities and she's given up a lot to support me being in this job. We've had a couple of moves and the hours aren't real regular. And at times the job has to come first, depending what's going on." Jack puffed on his cigar. "Tonight's an example. She wants me to talk to a headhunter about some jobs with a couple of the big companies in the Twin Cities so we know where we'll be for a while."

"And it will be safer?" Cyrus asked.

"The job isn't that dangerous, but it would be safer to work a corporate job."

Cyrus started coughing, rolled the window down and spit outside. After clearing his throat, he said, "I feel bad about you guys taking care of me. I'm interfering with your vacation. Especially with you all just getting back together."

"Don't worry about it. The kids love having you around. You're teaching us all how to fish. It's like having their grandpa around."

The phone sounded out a warning to turn left onto highway twenty-two.

Jack turned and the headlights lit up the highway and about twenty feet of ditch on either side. A wall of trees lined the ditches. Jack watched for deer on either side. The road followed the gentle hills up and down and curved its way around lakes and farms. They hadn't seen any deer yet, but they did see a cat and a raccoon scurrying across the road and into the grassy ditch.

"Cyrus, I've been thinking about the events of the past couple of days and your stories."

"OK."

"There have been some crazy coincidences. Were they really just coincidences?"

"Like what?" Cyrus asked.

Jack glanced over at Cyrus to get a feel for what he might be thinking. Was he hiding something? "When we found you at the park getting beat up by Clint, coincidence. You had a metal detector and we'd just lost Julie's wedding ring in the lake, coincidence."

"Right. It's weird."

"A weird coincidence." Jack continued. "Looking for the ring we found the dog license and you had a story for how it got there and it came from a Hokanson dog." Jack paused. "I don't think that was a coincidence." Jack glanced at Cyrus again.

"You're right, that sounds even weirder."

Both Jack and Cyrus stared out the windshield as they drove down the highway.

"Did you find the ring?" Cyrus asked.

Jack nodded in the dark. "Yep, I pocketed it. I want to find a special time in the next few days to give it to her. Something to cement our being back together."

"I didn't know you were such a romantic," Cyrus said. "She might be mad you've kept it from her."

"Mr. Romantic, that's me," Jack answered. He waited a short time and then asked. "Did you plant the dog license in the lake?"

"How could I be sure you'd find it if I dropped it in the lake?" Cyrus asked.

"So you made up the story?" Jack asked.

"No," Cyrus replied. "Only the part about the dog attacking him and fighting in the lake. The rest of it, my dad running from her brothers, was true. Or at least what my mother told me."

"How did she know?"

Cyrus coughed again and took a sip of coffee. He took another puff on his cigar and blew it out the window. "My father wrote her letters. Sent them to a friend of hers to give to her so the family wouldn't know. He told her the story of that day in a letter. They never saw each other again, but he knew he had a son, me."

"You're just baiting me and Julie along?"

"I don't want to be a burden. I'm trying to get you and Angela engaged against them."

Them, the Hokansons, Jack thought. "You've got a hell of a family you're related to."

Their questions appeared to be answered. Jack and Cyrus sat in silence, each in their own thoughts.

Jack followed the county road, waiting for the phone to tell him when to turn again. One more major turn and then it should be a straight shot to Staples. He glanced at the time and sped up a little bit. He wanted to have time to get set up to watch the station when they got there.

. . .

JACK DROVE over the train tracks and stopped at the traffic light. He'd looked at some satellite map images before they left the cabin. Things looked like they did in the image. The train tracks ran east and west, parallel to highway ten on the south edge of Staples. To his left was the brick train station, the lone building on the south side of the highway between the highway and the railroad tracks.

There was a small parking lot on the west side of the station, but Jack didn't think they should park there. It was too small and they'd stick out. He planned to park across the highway from the train station in the bank parking lot. He could see the parking lot and station from there.

The light turned green and he turned left. Highway ten ran right through Staples. It was two lanes in each direction, with a small concrete median dividing the east and west lanes.

Cyrus snored in the seat next to him. Jack pulled into the bank parking lot and faced the car south so they could watch the Amtrak station. He rolled down his window all the way and turned off the car.

The train should be coming through in about fifteen minutes. There were two cars in the parking lot. Couples stood by their cars, talking. Dakota oil field workers getting dropped off? Who else would be getting on the train at Staples at one twenty-six in the morning?

Jack reached over and slipped the small box of cigars out of Cyrus' pocket. The lighter was in the tray between the seats. Jack lit the cigar and waited.

If they didn't spot anything here, they'd need to race the train to Detroit Lakes. Jack checked the map on his phone. The train tracks paralleled highway ten all the way there from Staples. Sixty-three miles according to the map.

The train blew its horn and the signal lights at the crossing he'd passed coming into town lit up and started ringing its bells. Jack's phone said 1:24.

Cyrus stirred in the seat. He blew out a breath and sat up straighter in his seat. "What's going on?" he asked.

"The train's coming in to Staples. Right on time. I see a couple of people across the way, waiting to get on. We'll see if anyone gets off. If not, we need to hightail it to DL. The train schedule says it gets there at 2:22 and we're an hour drive away on the highway."

The silver Empire Builder with its red, white and blue stripes slipped slowly past the depot building and stopped.

"I could use a drink of water," Cyrus said.

"We don't have time now. I think those people will load quickly and it will leave. You'll have to settle for cold coffee if you have any left."

They watched people saying goodbye and getting in their cars. It didn't appear that anybody got off. A quick stop, as Jack had expected. The train blew its horn.

Jack figured he could push eighty miles per hour and maybe not get stopped by a highway patrol car. If they could do that, it gave him fifteen minutes of lead-time over the train.

"Hang on, it's time to boogie." Jack drove forward over the sidewalk and bumped over the curb onto the highway.

CHAPTER EIGHTEEN

It was a race. Sixty-three miles along highway ten to the next stop, Detroit Lakes, and they had to get there before the train if they wanted time to see people waiting for the train or getting off the train. Jack looked to his left as they pulled ahead of the Amtrak engine on a parallel course to the highway. According to the train schedule, they were going to be in Detroit Lakes in less than an hour.

"Cyrus, I need you to watch for highway patrol along here." Jack sped up and watched the speedometer move from sixty to seventy and then eighty. "We need to win the race to Detroit Lakes."

"Giddy-up, let's go." Cyrus lit his cigar and sat up in his seat. "You think we'll see something there since they weren't at this stop?"

"I'd put money on it. The FBI's intel is usually pretty good." The highway was empty. No headlights ahead of them. Only the light of the train in the rearview mirror.

"Who do you think it's going to be?"

"It wouldn't surprise me if it's Clint."

"Wishful thinking?"

Jack shook his head. He thought back over the past few days, what he'd learned about the Hokansons and their past, Clint's reputation, the overdoses. "If it's not the Hokansons I don't know who it would be. They wouldn't allow someone else to profit off the drugs in their county."

They sped along the highway in silence for a while when Cyrus spoke.

"So you think you're going to leave the FBI?" Cyrus asked.

Jack shrugged. "I really can't decide. I was supposed to talk with this headhunter, but I keep putting it off." Jack checked his rearview mirror and continued, "the private sector has some advantages: better pay, vacation, stuff like that. Using my FBI knowledge and experience for corporate security. Not getting shot at. Quite a few of my peers have left. They like it."

"Not everyone leaves," Cyrus said. "How do you feel?"

Jack paused a second before answering. How did he feel? He wasn't sure. He'd been a special agent for fifteen years and always thought he'd be one until mandatory retirement. "It's that career versus family thing. What's the best for both? I love the FBI and what I do. But I agreed to talk with the recruiter."

A town was up ahead. The sign said New York Mills. A traffic light flashed a yellow warning light. Jack debated how much to slow down. A glance in the rearview mirror showed the bright headlight of the engine behind them, but if he had to stop or slow down too much, they'd catch up. He lifted his foot from the gas and the SUV immediately began to slow. He scanned up ahead. "You see a cop or highway patrol or anything?"

"I think you need to slow down a little, but I don't see anybody," Cyrus answered.

Jack let the SUV continue to roll on its own, his foot hovering over the brake. He checked again in the rearview mirror. No cars behind him. The train headlight continued to follow.

Reaching the far end of town, Jack accelerated again. He glanced at the clock. They were about half-way there. Still good to go. As long as they could keep up the speed, they should be there with time ahead of the train.

"Hey, what do you think of the police chief, Angela?" Jack asked.

Cyrus didn't respond right away.

"Think we can trust her?"

"You know," Cyrus started, he paused a beat, the SUV sped forward. "I've been thinking about that. I think she's in a tough situation. Not sure how she got there. How'd she get to be chief if she's not on the Hokanson's side?" He paused again. "But she seems to care for the people of her town. She hasn't done anything to show us she's on the dark side. I think she's trustworthy, wants to do what's right."

Jack didn't respond. He mulled over what Cyrus said and thought over the last couple of days.

"I like her," Cyrus said.

"Yeah, me too," Jack responded.

WHEN THEY REACHED Detroit Lakes they had to slow down. Traffic lights cycled and they hit a red light. There was plenty of traffic on the roads with bars closing and police out. Jack hoped they didn't hit a DUI check and get stopped. If there was one, it would probably be for traffic going the other way, away from the bars.

"The Amtrak station should be right up here. I'll find a place to park where we can see what's going on," Jack said.

He turned right off the highway and then took a left at the next block. A few people were standing around outside the station, waiting for the train. Jack pulled into a parking spot at the Amtrak station, lowered the windows and turned off the car. "I think we have about five minutes. At least we beat it here."

"Look." Cyrus pointed at a truck coming up the street towards the station. A white panel van with the Hokanson logo on the side.

Jack slumped over to the right, trying not to be seen. "And look who's driving. It's your cousin."

"Cousin twice removed," Cyrus answered. "Son of a bitch."

The truck rolled by.

"I don't think he saw us," Jack said.

"He's too stupid to even think someone would be here watching."

"They could be picking someone up, getting a shipment for the concert."

Cyrus coughed and responded. "Could be, I guess. If that shipment is drugs to sell to the concert goers."

The train let loose a soft blast of its horn and pulled into the station. Jack reached up and adjusted his review mirror to get a view of the truck. He reached out and adjusted the side mirror as well. Once the train stopped, people started migrating towards the platform to pick up passengers or to get ready to board.

"He's pulled the truck up to the curb," Jack said.

"There he goes," Cyrus said.

"I'm going to follow him. You watch the truck." Jack opened the door, jumped out.

"Don't let him see you," Cyrus warned.

"I'm a trained professional," Jack answered. He softly closed the door and trotted across the street to follow Clint.

Jack helped an older woman carry a suitcase to blend into the crowd a little and rounded the corner of the station. Clint walked up ahead, oblivious to anything around him. He appeared to be looking for someone. Jack carried the bag to the door of the station and held the door open for the woman.

Clint stopped and raised his hand to catch somebody's attention. Jack stood in the doorway of the station and watched. A twenty-something woman walked up to Clint. She carried a backpack on her back. She and Clint talked. She removed the pack and set it on the ground between her and Clint. Clint gave her a small paper bag and she walked away in the opposite direction. Clint bent over and hefted the backpack onto his shoulder.

Jack ducked into the station and stepped along the wall to avoid being seen. He pretended to look at some of the Detroit Lakes area attraction pamphlets on the wall and looked out the glass door to watch Clint.

Clint walked by, wrestling his arms through the straps of the backpack. Jack watched him until he was out of sight and then he quickly went out the door.

His phone buzzed in his pocket. He pulled it out. A call from Cyrus. "Yeah?"

"He's coming back. Someone from the station wheeled a couple of boxes out and set them at the back of the van."

"I'm just behind him a bit. Around the corner of the building. I'll be right there." Jack ended the call, peeked around the corner. Clint wasn't in sight, so Jack jogged down the platform along the tracks and then cut over across the parking lot towards his SUV.

At the street, he slowed and calmly walked to his car and got in. He looked into the rearview mirror. Cyrus was twisted around watching out through the back window. "What's he doing?" Jack asked.

"Looks like he threw the boxes and backpack into the back end of the van."

"He got the pack from a girl getting off the train," Jack

said. "Just like I saw a guy getting on the train with a backpack the night before I left for vacation. That one was full of illegal drugs and pharmaceuticals."

Jack started the truck and waited for Clint to drive by. "Let's see where he's going."

STAYING FAR ENOUGH BACK SO Clint wouldn't get suspicious, Jack followed the van west on County Road 10, the main street through Detroit Lakes. The traffic was light at this time of the night or morning. Whichever it was. They didn't have any cars between them. Bright street lights and stop lights lit up an intersection ahead. "He'll turn south there to Pelican," Jack said. It was the main intersection with Highway 59 running south.

"What if the light turns red?" Cyrus asked. "We can't pull right up behind him. He might see us in his mirrors."

Jack let up on the gas and let the car decelerate, giving them a little more space. "I'll just drive by and double back if I have to."

"You've done this before. I forgot. You're a trained professional."

"A few times," Jack said.

Clint signaled and pulled into the left turn lane. The light was green. He turned south onto the two-lane highway. The light turned yellow.

Jack slowed.

"Go," Cyrus said.

Jack stopped for the red light. His turn signal blinking for a left turn. Clint's taillights moved from the lights of the intersection into the dark towards Pelican Rapids. "We'll give him some space. Didn't want him glancing back as we rushed through the light."

Cyrus lit another cigar and blew the smoke out the

window. Jack waited for a count of five. "See anybody?" he asked.

"Just us and Clint getting away," Cyrus said.

Jack turned left on the red light and followed Clint south into the dark.

CLINT DROVE AHEAD of them about a half of a mile. He followed the speed limit. Jack held back and matched his speed to keep a steady distance back. Far enough back to not get Clint's attention. They drove along the two-lane highway slightly curving between hills and lakes. The moon glistened on the water.

A pair of headlights became visible as a car came over a hill heading towards them. Jack checked his speed and distance from Clint.

The headlights got brighter as they got closer. When the car was about fifty yards ahead of them, Cyrus said, "Cop."

The car buzzed by going the other direction. Jack read the decal on the side of the car as it was lit up from his headlights. "Sheriff car," Jack said. He watched the car in his side mirror. The brake lights came on and it pulled a u-turn on the highway. Jack reached for his phone, hit the redial and put the phone on speaker.

A groggy voice answered, "Hello. Do you know what time it is?"

"Angela, wake up," Jack said. "I don't have much time, so listen. Cyrus and I are following Clint from Detroit Lakes towards Pelican. He's in a white Hokanson panel van. I want you to follow him and see where he goes."

Angela cleared her throat. "Why do you need me?"

The sheriff's car pulled up closer behind Jack. "I think we're going to be delayed by a deputy so we can't stay with

Clint." The lights from the sheriff's car came on, the flashing lights reflecting in the cab of the SUV.

"Shit," Cyrus said.

"He's pulling us over now. Don't say anything. I'm going to drop the phone between the seat and the door so you can hear. Just follow Clint when he comes through town. Call me when you're free. We may be sleeping at the cabin. We've been up all night." Jack turned down the volume and slid the phone between the seat and the door. He signaled and pulled over onto the shoulder of the highway and stopped. He watched Clint's taillights pull farther ahead until they disappeared over the hill.

Jack pulled his driver's license out and held it in one hand. He put both hands on the steering wheel. "Just keep your hands out where he can see them," Jack said to Cyrus. "He's approaching the car," he said so Angela could hear.

The deputy stopped outside the car.

"Everything OK?" Jack asked.

The deputy bent over and looked at the two of them in the SUV. "What are you two doing out so late tonight?" he asked.

Jack kept his hand on the wheel. "My friend here couldn't sleep, so we decided to go for a little drive."

"You been drinking?" the deputy asked.

"No sir," Jack answered.

"I think you might have been swerving a little on the road. Let me see your license."

Jack handed the deputy his license without responding and put his hand back on the steering wheel.

"You guys sit tight. I'll be right back."

"Asshole," Cyrus whispered.

Jack directed his voice down towards the phone. "Cyrus thinks the deputy is an asshole in case you didn't hear him. I think we're going to be delayed here until Clint is far enough ahead. So, we need you to follow him. Call us when you're done." Jack saw the deputy in the mirror. "The deputy's coming back. Talk to you later."

When the deputy got to the side of the car, he handed Jack's license back to him. "You guys be careful tonight. Follow the speed limit and watch for deer. They've been active on this road lately."

Jack took the license. "Thanks." He signaled left to get back on the highway, put the car in drive and slowly drove away, leaving the deputy behind.

CHAPTER NINETEEN

The headlights from their car blazed a trail ahead of them as they headed south on Highway 59. Jack checked his rearview mirror. The deputy had turned around and headed north towards Detroit Lakes, the direction he'd been going when he pulled them over.

"Did he know you're FBI?" Cyrus asked.

Jack answered, "I think he knew, but not from running my plates or my license. It doesn't show up there."

"And you didn't tell him."

"No reason to," Jack paused, "and kind of a test. I was curious if he'd show his hand." Jack reached down and found his phone from where he'd stashed it next to the seat. "I'm sure he pulled us over to keep us from following Clint. We'll see what Angela has to say after she tails him."

Jack kept the speedometer at just above fifty-five miles per hour. He didn't think there'd be another deputy out here looking for him, but he wanted to be sure he wasn't speeding if there was.

Cyrus pulled out his box of Swisher Sweets and lit one. Jack stuck his hand out. Cyrus handed him the lit cigar and shook another out of the box for himself. They both smoked their cigars, blew smoke out the windows and watched the road ahead of them.

"So, you think the gold from your story is real?" Jack asked.

Cyrus turned and looked at Jack. "What?" he asked.

Jack repeated his question a little louder to be heard over the wind coming in through the windows. "Is the gold real?"

"Are you asking if my dear departed mother is a liar?"

Jack smiled and shook his head. "No. Never. But is there gold hidden somewhere out here? Have you found it?"

"I haven't found anything. I believe there is. My daddy just hid it too well to be found."

"Do you think we can find it?" Jack asked.

"I've been looking so I can tell you where it isn't."

Jack laughed.

Cyrus took another drag from his cigar and let the wind suck the smoke away as he slowly exhaled. "If I keep looking, I'll find it the last place I look."

Jack laughed again. "Well, that's something." His cell phone rang. He checked to see who was calling and answered it. "Hey, Angela. Cyrus and I are just about to Pelican. We'll pick up some food and coffee at the gas station." He listened and then answered. "Yep. We'll see you at your office in fifteen minutes."

JACK PARKED in the police station parking lot and he and Cyrus went in to find Angela. In the office, someone Jack hadn't met was at the desk. "Hey," Jack said. "We're here to see the Chief."

"She's in her office," the person responded and nodded back towards the door.

The door was open. Angela sat at her desk wearing a

Minnesota Twins t-shirt with her hair pulled back into a ponytail.

Jack walked in, followed by Cyrus. "Morning," Jack said. He put a coffee cup on the desk for her and a container of mini-powdered donuts. "Cream and sugar just as you requested."

"You guys don't look too bad for being up all night," Angela said. She took the cover off of the To-Go coffee cup, blew across the coffee to cool it and took a sip. "Thanks for the coffee."

Cyrus pulled up a chair and Jack sat in the one in front of her desk. Cyrus took a bite of a donut, leaving a white ring of powdered sugar around his lips.

Jack grabbed one, took a bite and then a drink of his coffee. He closed his eyes, swallowed and licked his lips. "That's pretty good."

"Breakfast of champions," Cyrus said.

Jack took another drink of his coffee. "Sorry for the early morning wake up call."

"So, who pulled you over?" Angela asked.

"It was a sheriff's deputy. Name tag said, Ashby or something like that."

"He didn't ticket you?"

"Nope. He was just slowing us down, I think."

Angela took another drink of her coffee and grabbed a donut.

"What'd you find out?" Jack asked.

"I followed the truck as it went through town. It went out to their ranch."

Jack thought about the night; Clint picking up a backpack from the girl getting off the train, then him driving to the ranch. "I don't know what I can report back to my team other than something got delivered." He leaned forward to emphasize his point. "But I think you've got a drug problem in this county and the Hokansons are heavily involved. Or, at least Clint is."

"I know," Angela said. "If it's dirty cops, you'll help? But, if not, I'm on my own."

"Or you work with the county sheriff," Jack said.

"Not unless I know I can trust him and his deputies," Angela answered.

"I guess that's what we need to figure out," Jack said. "You tell me what you need."

"I'll think about it."

They each grabbed another donut. Powdered sugar covered the desk and speckled their shirts.

"Why'd you buy these?" Angela asked. "They're making a mess."

Jack answered with a donut in his mouth. Powdered sugar puffed out into the air. "I like them."

After they finished their donuts and coffee, Angela asked what they were going to do next. Jack looked at his watch and glanced at Cyrus. "You tired?" he asked.

"I don't think I could sleep now," Cyrus answered.

Jack turned back to Angela. "Maybe we'll go fishing. Want to join us?"

"Thanks for the offer," she answered. "But I have to work."

Jack used a napkin to sweep the powdered sugar on the desk into a pile and then off the edge into his hand. He dumped it in his empty coffee cup and stood up. "When you figure out what you want to do, you let me know. I'll think about it while we're fishing and maybe after a nap. I don't like these Hokansons," Jack turned to Cyrus, "sorry to bad mouth your family."

Cyrus gave him the bird sticking up one of his gnarled fingers. "My family by accident. Once and twice removed I told you."

Smiling, Jack turned back to Angela, "and not sure if we know if there's anybody in the Sheriff's department you can trust." He tossed his coffee can in the trash can next to her desk and helped Cyrus up from his chair. "We're going fishing. We'll talk to you later today."

Cyrus stopped at the door and turned back to Angela. "And you be careful," he said.

CHAPTER TWENTY

It was still dark as Jack and Cyrus drove south out of Pelican Rapids. Jack checked his watch for the time. Just after five. "You tired?" Jack asked.

"No," Cyrus answered. "I think I'm getting my second wind after those donuts and coffee. Did you have something in mind?"

"I don't know if I want to head out fishing in the dark," Jack said.

"Sun comes up around six-thirty."

Jack drove ahead in the dark. This vacation wasn't quiet and boring like he thought it would be. He's staking out Amtrak, the Hokansons and the drugs, Angela, who he thinks he can trust, and the old man sitting next to him, Cyrus and his gold. "Think Angela can handle the Hokansons?" he asked.

"Yeah, for now. I like her," Cyrus said. "She's tough."

They got to the turn to the cabin. "Keep going straight," Cyrus said.

Jack canceled the turn signal and checked the rearview mirror. There was nobody behind them. "Where're we going?"

"We're going to talk gold. Civil War gold."

JACK FOLLOWED CYRUS' directions and turned left into a small gravel parking lot. A sign by the entrance said Lida Cemetery. He parked the car at the edge of the lot. "OK, what are we doing here? I didn't bring a shovel."

"Does your phone have the flashlight in it?"

"Yep," Jack answered.

Cyrus opened his door. "Bring it. We'll probably need it."

Jack shone a light ahead of them in the grass. Cyrus hobbled along. "Where are we going?" Jack asked.

"I haven't visited Mom since I came back." Cyrus led Jack ahead and up a small hill to a simple headstone. Cyrus leaned on it and caught his breath. He pulled out a cigar and lit it. "Want one?"

"Not now." Jack shined the light on it. There was a name, Gerta Hokanson.

"This is my mom. This is where the story of the gold started for me. She told me the stories I've shared with you about my dad and her family."

"But she didn't tell you where the gold was?" Jack asked.

"I don't know if she knew. Members of the family all got some when she was young. She used hers to buy the island on South Lida. The island straight out from your cabin. And to build the house." Cyrus laughed. "You've seen it when we go by the island. The house is almost falling down, now."

"That's hers? Yours?"

"She bought it to get away from her family. To have a place of her own. Her brother used his money to get involved in bootlegging during prohibition bringing booze down from Canada."

"And there was more gold?" Jack asked.

"That was the story growing up. There was more that was kept for an emergency."

"And your dad stole it."

Cyrus smiled. "That's the story. He stole it, left town, went in the military and the secret of where he put the gold went with him."

"He didn't tell your mom?"

"Not that I knew. She didn't tell me." Cyrus coughed, cleared his throat and spit in the grass.

Jack checked out the headstones around them. "No other family here?"

Cyrus shook his head and puffed his cigar. "Just her. She didn't want to be with the rest of the family." He put his fingers to his lips, touched the headstone and started shuffling down the hill towards the car. "Thanks for bringing me here."

JACK PULLED out of the parking lot. The sky was growing lighter. "Time to go fishing?"

"Might as well see if you can catch something."

"You're my guide. I can blame you if I don't catch anything"

Cyrus laughed and Jack joined him. After spending almost the entire night together in the car, they'd been through a lot and were getting comfortable with each other, trusting each other.

"But, what about the gold? Where do you think it is?" Jack asked.

"Jackie boy, you getting bit by the bug?"

"No, I'm a trained detective. I'm always trying to solve the mystery. I can't leave it alone." Jack headed for the cabin, the sky to the east growing brighter.

"You said he swam from the island across the lake to the

west side. What if he dropped it in the lake because he couldn't make it across with it?"

"Then it's at the bottom of the lake and will never be found."

Jack drove and thought some more. "I think he was too smart to try and swim the lake with it."

"I don't know if I have any more clues for you," Cyrus answered.

Jack turned off the county road onto the gravel road leading to the cabin. "Maybe fishing will help us think of something."

CHAPTER TWENTY-ONE

Otto and Clint sat at the island in the kitchen. Otto poured coffee into a couple of mugs. Hanna walked in, wiping the sleep from her eyes. "What are you doing up?" Otto asked.

"I had to pee and heard you guys talking. What are you guys doing up so early?"

Otto got up and walked to the cupboard for another mug. "Coffee?"

Hanna sat at an empty stool at the island. "No, just some ice water, please. I'm trying to stay away from coffee for the baby."

"That's good, sis," Clint said. "Keep the incubator clean. I'll have some for you." He poured some more coffee into his own mug.

Otto set the glass of ice water in front of Hanna and sat. "I was just telling Clint that I got a call from Deputy Ashby. He pulled Agent Miller and Cyrus over this morning. He said it looked like they were following Clint on his way back from DL. They weren't too far behind him on the highway."

"I think it might have just been a coincidence," Clint said.

"I didn't see anybody at the depot watching me and didn't see them behind me."

Hanna leaned forward, elbows on the island. "He is an FBI agent. He knows something about stakeouts and tails, I assume," she said to Clint. "It was no coincidence. What did Ashby say?" she asked her father.

"He pulled them over for some bullshit reason. Delayed them enough to give Clint some time to get out ahead of them," Otto said. "Then he sent them on their way."

"What are we going to do?" Hanna asked.

Otto took a drink of coffee. "Clint's made the delivery to the ranch. We get this to work and set up some more festivals across the Midwest next summer and we're set to distribute and launder the cash from Wisconsin to Montana. We can control the Midwest. If we prove this works, we can forget about the Mexican and Hmong gangs from Minneapolis and Chicago for supplies. We'll get the attention of the Canadian distributors. It's an easier transport from up north."

"But what about Agent Miller and Cyrus?" Hanna asked.

"We keep an eye on them. Be aware they're watching us, but I don't think they really have an idea what's going on," Otto answered.

Clint slammed down his mug. Coffee splashed onto the island. "Damn it. Why don't we just go find the gold? Give me some time with Cyrus and I'll get him to tell me where it is."

Otto grabbed a washcloth from the sink and wiped up the spilled coffee. "That's just a story. My great grandfather had some coins he brought back from the war. He spent some to get his booze running business up and running during prohibition and gave some to my grandfather and Cyrus' mother, but it wasn't a lot. Grandfather used some of his money to buy some land and Cyrus' mother bought the island

and built a house. But that's it. The drugs are real. This is now."

"I don't know," Clint said. "Why else is Cyrus hanging around here this summer?"

"He's dying," Otto said. "He's not looking for any gold. Now, you just focus on your drug distribution and keep an eye out for those two. Make sure they aren't following you around anymore."

CHAPTER TWENTY-TWO

The rising sun burned the mist off the lake. The trolling motor quietly pulled the boat through the water. The only other sounds were the chirping of birds and the distant hum of the outboard motors of other people going out to fish. Jack watched the depth finder looking for the depression Cyrus said was south of the bog.

"It's getting deeper," Jack said.

"Turn off the motor and I'll drop the anchor."

Cyrus slipped the anchor into the water. The rope stretched out from the bow of the boat and Cyrus tied it off on the cleat. "This should be a good spot for Crappies. After finding the spot, the next secret is to find what depth they're at and what they're hungry for."

Cyrus handed Jack a fishing pole. A red and white bobber was attached to the line, a green and yellow-headed jig attached to the end. "Why don't you start with a minnow. We could cast and retrieve, but let's start with this. Set the bobber so about six feet of line hangs down from it and throw it out there. Just reel it in real slow. And throw it out again. Repeat until you get a fish. I'll start with a leech over here."

Jack followed Cyrus' instructions and cast the line out away from the boat. "Thanks for the tips, Cyrus. I'll impress the kids if I can get them to catch some fish."

Cyrus nodded and concentrated on lighting up his cigar. With a couple of puffs, he had it lit. "Too bad the kids have such a hard time getting up this early. It's a beautiful time of day."

Jack and Cyrus had snuck out of the cabin this morning without waking anybody, except Vince. Jack left Vince out to explore around the cabin. The last Jack saw, Vince was wading through the water along the shore looking for frogs.

It was a beautiful morning. Jack watched the bobber float on the surface of the lake and thought about the last couple of days. Sitting in a boat, fishing, matched his visions of vacation. But there were a lot of other things going on he hadn't dreamed of for his vacation.

"Cyrus, what are you doing here?"

"Fishing."

"Really. Why did you come back to Pelican Rapids?"

Cyrus inhaled his cigar and sputtered and coughed, the smoke drifting up into the morning sky. He coughed some more, cleared his throat and spit into the lake. "Maybe I shouldn't smoke these things," he said. "But, I love them." He reeled in his line, checked his bait and cast it back into the lake.

"I'm dying, Jack. I came home to say goodbye." Cyrus reeled in his line a few cranks. "I have to thank you and Julie for letting me spend some time with your family. I've really enjoyed the last couple of days."

"You're welcome," Jack responded. "I'm sorry to hear about your health."

"Yeah, I'm old. One of my biggest regrets is not bringing Ruby back here over the years to enjoy it. It's such a special place in the summer."

Jack waited and let Cyrus continue.

"When she died, I realized that I missed that with her and blamed the Hokansons for me staying away." Cyrus looked out over the lake. "And I blame myself."

Looking out over the lake, Jack thought about his own family and their vacation here. "You know, everybody talks about going to the lake. We never did it, but I'm starting to understand the allure."

Cyrus cast his line out again. "Otter Tail County has about a thousand of the ten thousand lakes Minnesota claims. They're all pretty nice, but this one is extra special. It's quiet, beautiful and the fact that Maplewood State Park is here along the east shore is preserving all of that."

Jack cast his own line out again to a new spot on the lake. As he slowly reeled the line back in, he thought about what Cyrus said about why he came back this summer. He thought Cyrus told him part of the answer, but there was more to why he was back other than to reminisce.

"Hey, I'm getting a bite," Jack said. His bobber moved around the surface of the lake, partially submerging and popping back up. He was excited, like a little kid catching his first fish of their vacation.

"Tighten the line just a little," Cyrus said. "When it goes under all the way, set the hook and reel it in."

Jack stood up and concentrated on the bobber and the feel of the fishing rod in his hands. The fish pulled the bobber under and Jack jerked up on the rod. The fish pulled the rod tip towards the water as it fought against the tug of the hook and the line.

"You got him. Now reel it in slowly. Keep tension on the line so the hook doesn't slip out of his mouth. He's fighting like a keeper," Cyrus said.

The tip of the rod dipped again towards the water and

Jack fought against it, moving the fish towards the boat. "He's almost here," he said. "I see him."

"Don't lose him. That's lunch or supper."

Jack pulled the fish towards the surface next to the boat.

Cyrus offered some more instructions. "Now, hold the rod up with one hand and reach down and put your other hand down. Put your thumb in this mouth and grip his lower lip. Crappie don't have sharp teeth."

Following Cyrus' orders, Jack bent over and lifted the fish out of the water.

"That's a nice fish. Put it in the live well and we'll see if we can get some more for lunch."

Jack removed the hook from the fish's lip and held it against the measuring board to see if it was big enough to keep. "Guess we better catch some more," he said.

He put his fish in the live well and hit the button on the console to add some water. Waiting for it to fill, he glanced up at a jet ski that zoomed by the mouth of the bay. It was early for a joy ride on a jet ski.

"I hate those things," Cyrus said. "They're too loud, especially this early in the morning."

"I'd swear that was Clint heading towards the cabin," Jack said.

Cyrus started reeling in his line. "We better go check. What reason does he have to be over here so early in the morning?"

"Bring up the trolling motor. I'll haul up the anchor," Jack said.

They completed their tasks and Cyrus sat down. "Let's go."

Jack turned the key and the motor started with a roar.

With the throttle pushed to the limit, the bow of the boat lifted out of the water tilting towards the sky, obscuring their view. The bow dropped as the boat planed out and soon they were heading back to the cabin at forty miles per hour.

The wind grabbed the brim of Jack's ball cap and it sailed into the water. He ignored it and pushed forward on the throttle that was at its limit, trying to make the boat go faster.

Exiting the bay, Jack turned left towards the cabin, cutting across the main part of the lake. He scanned the shore to see where the jet ski had gone. He spotted it bobbing in the lake in front of their cabin and pointed it out to Cyrus.

He didn't see Clint, but knew he was there. A hundred yards from shore, Jack eased back on the throttle and the boat slowed, the water helping to lower the speed. Clint came running down the hill from the cabin, with Vince barking at his heels. He jumped into the lake and climbed up on the jet ski.

Jack tried to maneuver the boat into his path, but Clint accelerated around them. Jack's initial reflex was to follow, but he was worried about his family. He tore his gaze from Clint racing across the lake and turned towards the cabin. He started to steer the boat towards shore when Julie appeared at the top of the hill.

"What's all the noise down here?" she asked.

Jack called up, "You all OK? Clint Hokanson was just here."

Julie gave him a thumbs-up.

"We'll be right back," he yelled. He sat down and gripped the throttle. "Hang on, Cyrus."

THE BOAT ZIPPED across the lake, following the wake the jet ski left on the calm surface. Jack pushed the throttle to its limit and tried to push it further.

Clint had crossed the line, showing up at his cabin where his family was sleeping. Jack was going to force Clint back over the line. Way back.

The jet ski was pulling farther away. They couldn't match the speed with the boat. The speedometer was steady at 45 mph. If they stayed close, they'd catch Clint when he got to his destination.

They flew by the island and the narrow that led into the second big part of the lake as they followed him north. The only sound Jack heard was the roar of the boat's engine and the wind buffeting his ears. Cyrus sat on his left, his hand grasping the windshield support as they hurled across the lake.

Clint was heading straight for the culvert under the road to the big lake. Jack knew where he was going. Home. To dad.

They closed the distance a little as Clint slowed the jet ski to pass through the culvert.

Jack wasn't slowing. He calculated his speed and distance, trying to determine when he should slow the boat and raise the motor and how fast they could be going and make it through. It wasn't windy. If he held true, they may just coast through and then speed up again when they made it to the other side.

Cyrus tapped him on the leg. "Slow down," he yelled.

Jack maintained his grip on the throttle. Clint probably thought he lost them going through the culvert. One hundred yards out, Jack played it through in his mind: cut the power, the weight of the boat against the water would slow them, push the button on the end of the throttle to raise the motor enough so it didn't hit the bottom, hold the boat steady, maybe scrape through on one side or the other. Once they were through, lower the motor and accelerate.

"Slow down, Jack. We'll never make it through going this fast!" Cyrus yelled again.

The culvert opening loomed ahead of them. They were aligned with the opening and still traveling at 45 mph. Eighty yards, fifty yards, forty yards.

"Jack!"

Jack cranked the steering wheel to the right and the boat swung in a tight arc, throwing a wave of water towards the rocky shore. Cyrus braced himself against the edge of the boat.

Jack knew where Clint was going. He could still beat that son of a bitch home.

JACK AIMED the boat about 200 feet ahead to the public boat launch ramp. With the boat slipped into idle, the bow bumped into the bottom of the lake at the base of the ramp. Jack jumped over the side into the shallow water. He gave the boat a push away from shore and took off across the gravel parking lot of the public ramp. He sprinted up the road, ignoring his soggy shoes. He'd beat Clint to the dock since he had to go around shallow areas and reed beds to get there.

It was time to let Clint and Otto know they had to leave him and his family alone.

Jack reached the compound entrance framed by the stone pillars and pounded up the blacktop driveway. At the house, he veered left toward the lake. He was winded, but he ran across the lawn and the lake came into view.

"Agent Miller," he heard someone yell from the deck behind him. It was probably Otto. He'd deal with him later. Jack continued towards the lake and the docks.

JACK RAN across the lawn and onto the dock as Clint was getting off the jet ski.

Clint looked at him, made a move like he was going to go

back to the jet ski, then stood his ground on the dock. He curled his hands into fists and set his feet, ready for a fight.

Without slowing, Jack took a couple more steps and launched himself through the air. His shoulder caught Clint just above the waist. He wrapped his arms around the back of Clint's legs like a football tackle and they both flew off the end of the dock.

They hit the water and Jack felt Clint pounding on his back. They were both underwater and Jack spun to get the advantage, like a gator with its prey. Jack's lungs burned, wanting to take a breath. Whoever needed to breathe first would lose. He squeezed his shoulder into Clint's midsection to drive the air from his lungs to get him to give up. Two taps on Jack's back and then no more struggle told him Clint was done.

Jack loosened his grip and slid down past Clint's waist to his ankles, pushing him towards the surface. Then he searched for the bottom with his feet and stood up. He found himself standing with his head above the water, Clint's feet in his grasp.

Clint was on his back, sucking in air and swearing at Jack to let him go.

Jack started walking to shore, dragging Clint, floating along behind him. Clint swore at him some more and Jack raised Clint's feet in the air, forcing his head below the water.

When he reached about waist-deep in the water, he stopped. Otto stood on the shore, a uniformed deputy standing beside him.

"You want to let him go, sir?" the deputy asked.

"Didn't we meet this morning?" Jack asked.

"Agent Miller, I think you can let him go now," Otto added.

Water dripped from Jack's hair down his face. His wet

shirt clung to his skin. He lifted Clint's feet into the air one final time, forcing his head under the water and shoved him out into the lake.

"Jack, you OK?"

Jack glanced back and saw Cyrus sitting in the boat about twenty feet from the end of the dock. He gave a wave of his hand to let him know all was fine. He knew Cyrus wouldn't hear him above the noise of the idling motor.

Behind him, he heard Clint splashing and yelling. "I'm going to get you, you mother."

"Settle down Clint," Otto yelled. "We'll get this all figured out."

The deputy took a step forward. "So, can you let us know what brought you to the Hokanson's property this morning and why you and Clint are fighting in the lake?"

Jack stood his ground in the water and stared at Otto.

"Did you hear me, sir?" the deputy asked.

Cyrus started yelling from out on the lake. "Otto, you hear me? Otto." Cyrus stood up in the boat. "That good for nothin' son of yours was sneaking around the Miller's cabin this morning. We caught him and chased him over here. I don't know what you're up to, but it's ..."

Cyrus didn't finish his sentence. He swayed in place and then it looked like his knees gave out and he went down in the boat.

"You." Jack pointed at the deputy. "Call an ambulance." Then he turned and dove into the water and swam towards the boat.

When he reached the boat, Jack reached up and grabbed the side of the boat and pulled himself up to peer over the side. He saw Cyrus lying in the bottom of the boat. "Cyrus, can you hear me?" There was no response. Jack didn't know if he could haul himself into the boat. The boat was still idling.

He thought about trying to knock the throttle into gear. But what would he do if he couldn't get it steered towards shore?

He lowered himself back into the lake and swam to the front of the boat. There was a rope from a ring at the front edge of the boat that ran along the side and into the boat, where it was tied to a cleat. Jack grabbed the line and started kicking and stroking with his free arm to pull the boat towards shore.

When the water was shallow enough, Jack stood and reached into the boat and turned off the motor. He pushed the button on the throttle to tilt the motor up so that he could push the boat closer to shore without the prop hitting the bottom. A glance told him Cyrus was still out. He still had color and Jack could now hear the shallow, rattled breathing. "Where's that ambulance?"

"It should be here soon." The deputy waded out into the lake to help Jack.

"Hold on to the boat," Jack said.

Jack lifted a leg up over the side of the boat and climbed in. He knelt next down in the boat. "Cyrus." Jack gently slapped Cyrus' cheeks. "Can you hear me?" He felt around Cyrus' head and then checked his arms and legs to make sure he hadn't hurt himself in his fall.

Cyrus inhaled deeply, turned his head and mumbled something.

"Cyrus, you're going to be OK. We've got an ambulance coming." He said to the deputy. "Pull the boat as close to shore as you can. I think we should get him out of the boat and lay him on the grass so the ambulance crew can check him out as soon as they get here."

Jack wrestled Cyrus' limp body up and over the side of the boat and handed him to the deputy to hold while he climbed over the side. They both carried him to shore and set him down in the grass. The faint sound of the ambulance sirens sounded through the air. Otto and Clint stood on the shore, watching them. "Can one of you at least meet the ambulance and show them where we are?"

CHAPTER TWENTY-THREE

J ack sat at a picnic table at the Mill Pond behind the
Pelican Rapids Medical Center and closed his eyes. He
felt the warmth of the sun as it dried out his clothes.
The doctors told him they'd call him as soon as they were
done assessing Cyrus' condition. He felt guilty. He shouldn't
have put Cyrus in the position of chasing Clint and
challenging Otto, knowing his health issues.

And what kind of vacation was this? He had to get this
thing, whatever it was, with the Hokansons figured out so
that he could focus on the kids and Julie.

"Good morning." Angela stood across the table from Jack.
She was in her uniform, hair pulled back, sunglasses hiding
her eyes. "I brought you some coffee." She placed a To-Go
cup on the table in front of him. "Can I join you?"

"Thanks. Make yourself comfortable."

Angela sat down at the picnic table facing Jack and took a
sip of her coffee. "How's Cyrus?"

"I think he's good. Considering. I'm just waiting for them
to call me to let me know I can come in and see him." Jack

touched the phone on the table and looked at the screen, wondering when the call would come.

"The radio was busy this morning," Angela said. She waited for a second and then continued, "I thought you two would be sleeping in this morning after being out all night."

"After we left you we were both pretty wired, so we took a drive and when we got to the cabin, we decided to go fishing."

"What happened? I heard a call for the Sheriff to respond to a disturbance out at Hokanson's and then a call for an ambulance. Learned a little more when I called out to see if any assistance was needed."

Jack grabbed the coffee Angela brought him, peeled off the cover and blew on it before taking a sip. "It started out pretty quiet. Cyrus and I were out fishing. Then we found Clint sneaking around my cabin and chased him on his jet ski back to his place."

Angela didn't say anything. She just sat across from Jack, waiting for him to tell the story.

"Clint and I got into it and fell off the dock." Jack rubbed at the wet spots still showing on his shorts. "Cyrus got agitated yelling at Otto and collapsed in the boat. Now, I'm here waiting to hear how he's doing."

"Your phone survived?"

"Luckily it was in the boat when I fell into the water." Jack smiled.

"That's quite the morning. Does Julie know what's going on?"

"Yeah, I called her from the ambulance. I told her to stay at the cabin with the kids and that I'd update her when I knew more."

"You want me to send somebody over there? She feeling safe?" Angela asked.

After another sip of coffee. Jack answered. "She's fine.

Clint won't be back over there today, if ever. She'll keep the kids busy and keep an eye on them."

"If you change your mind, let me know," Angela said.

"You know what I could use?" Jack asked. "I could use some help in getting the boat back to our cabin from Hokansons."

"Already done. I talked to the Sheriff's deputy and we worked it out with one of my officers helping to shuttle him back to Hokansons."

"Thanks." Jack searched the sunglasses, seeing his reflection. Hard to get a read on what Angela was thinking without seeing her eyes. "I have to talk to the deputy that was out at the Hokansons sometime."

"I talked to him," Angela said.

"It was the same guy who stopped me and Cyrus last night."

"OK," Angela said. She sipped her coffee and looked away. Jack could see she was thinking about something. She turned back to face Jack. "Just stay away from the Hokansons. I think Otto wants things to quiet down. And he'll take care of Clint if he wasn't following Otto's orders."

Jack's phone pinged. He picked it up and checked the screen. "We can go see Cyrus," he said.

JACK HELD the door open and followed Angela into the room. Cyrus was in the bed, a tube connected to his arm and a sensor on his finger. The sun shone through the window.

Angela stopped and sucked in her breath.

Cyrus smiled weakly. "Chief," he said. "Miss me?" It came out softly and a little raspy.

"How are you?" Angela asked.

"I'm fine," Cyrus answered. He saw Jack and almost

started laughing. Instead, he started coughing. After he got it under control, he said, "You're still wet."

"I'm drying off. Nice to see you still have your sense of humor," Jack said.

Angela pulled a chair up next to the bed and sat down. She held Cyrus' hand. He smiled and gave her a clumsy wink.

"You gave us a little scare out there," Jack said, standing at the foot of the bed.

"Sorry about that." Cyrus coughed again. "I liked how you handled Clint in the lake, but I got a little excited and passed out."

"And a little pissed at Otto," Jack added.

"Yep," was all Cyrus said in reply.

"The Doc says if you're still good in a few hours and I promise to keep you calm, you can leave. And Julie says if I don't bring you back to the cabin, for us to watch you, she'll put me in the hospital."

Cyrus started coughing again. He reached for a white Styrofoam cup on the table by his bed. Angela leaned over, picked up the cup and held it while Cyrus guided the straw into his mouth. After a big sip, he leaned back against his pillows. "Don't make me laugh," he whispered.

"Are you OK?" Angela asked. She held his hand and rubbed his arm.

Cyrus nodded yes.

"Can I ask you some questions?" Angela glanced at Jack. He shrugged, wondering where she was going.

She turned back to Cyrus. "I think you need to clear things up about your relationship with Otto, why you're here in Pelican Rapids after being gone so long, why Clint was beating you up when we met."

Cyrus closed his eyes, inhaled deeply, blew it out and looked at Jack. Jack knew Cyrus was wondering what he should tell her. If he could trust her. There were things Jack was wondering too about Cyrus and his story. He knew there were things Cyrus hadn't told him. And with the condition Cyrus was in, something could happen and they'd never know. Jack nodded to tell Cyrus to go ahead.

Cyrus motioned for the water. Angela handed it to him and he took a big sip. "You might want to get comfortable, Jack. This might take a while," he said.

Jack pulled a chair over to the other side of the bed from Angela and sat down. "OK, I'm ready," he said.

"Where to start?" Cyrus asked. He didn't look at Angela or Jack. He stared at the wall past the foot of his bed. "My wife died last fall. Her name was Ruby. I think she died before me just to punish me."

Jack chuckled. At least Cyrus still had a sense of humor.

"I'm sick, as you can see. And I'm dying, which you probably figured out. Or the doctor told you. I decided that it was time to leave Chicago and come back to Pelican Rapids for the summer. It's small, simple, I always liked it here and they've got an OK hospital to deal with my issues." Cyrus took another sip of water. "I haven't been here since I was young. Never brought Ruby here. I regret that. She would've liked it here."

"I'm sorry," Angela said.

Cyrus shook his head. "It's my fault. I just stayed away after what happened with my mom and her family."

"So, why was Clint assaulting you in the park that day?" Angela asked.

"He was trying to get me to talk and to scare me off."

"From what?" she asked.

Jack guessed, "The drugs or the gold or both?"

Angela turned to Jack. "Gold?"

"I think both," Cyrus said. "I've been digging around a lot and I think I might've pushed a few buttons related to the drug business, so that might've had something to do with Clint's wanting to scare me off."

"What gold?" Angela asked.

Jack snickered and watched while Angela looked from him to Cyrus and back again. "Tell her the short version."

Cyrus used the bed control to tilt the bed a little higher, took another sip of his water, and repeated the story for Angela.

"How much is it?" Angela asked. "Where is it?"

"Slow down," Cyrus replied. "I don't even know if it exists. It's a family story. But Clint believes it. And I do. I've been looking for it this summer because if it does exist, I want to find it so the Hokansons can't have it."

"Where do you think it is?" Angela asked. "Where have you looked?"

"The Hokanson farm was where the State Park is now. He may have hidden it there, somewhere else in the park, in the lake, on the island. I don't know. I've looked around the park some, but I haven't found a thing."

Angela stood, walked to the window and looked outside. "What about the drugs?"

Cyrus cleared his throat and took another drink of water. "I didn't learn much. Enough to know Clint was involved in something. But, Jack's learned a lot more over the past couple of days."

Still standing at the window, Angela turned, leaned against the wall and asked, "And why do the Hokansons hate you so much."

Cyrus laughed. It triggered a coughing fit. After getting it under control, he answered, "There's no family love lost either way. I think I remind them of my mom, I threaten their criminal way of life, I'm not one of them."

A nurse knocked on the door and came into the room. "You

two need to leave. Cyrus needs his rest and a couple of more tests." She grabbed his chart from the foot of the bed and walked over to check the monitors next to the head of the bed.

"We'll be back in two hours to see if you're ready to go," Jack said to Cyrus.

"I'll be ready," Cyrus said.

"Maybe," the nurse said.

Angela stepped over and squeezed Cyrus' hand to say goodbye. "You take care of yourself," she said.

"If something happens to me, I want you guys to see the lawyer. The one across from the drugstore."

"You're going to be fine. We'll see you in a few hours," Jack said. He took a step towards the door. "Come on Angela. He needs some rest."

JACK STEPPED OUTSIDE into the sun. Angela followed him. "It's going to be a nice day," Jack said. He looked into the sky and felt the warmth on his face.

"You think he's going to be OK?" Angela asked.

"He's a tough old guy, but he knows his days are numbered," Jack said. "You heard him. He's sick. But he's where he wants to be."

"He's lucky to have you and your family looking after him."

"He doesn't have anyone else," Jack said. His cell phone buzzed and he took it out of his pocket. He was expecting to see a call from the headhunter, but the caller id told him the Special Agent in Charge was calling. "Just a second," he said to Angela. He answered the phone, "Hey boss."

It was a one-sided conversation with a lot of yes, sirs and no, sirs.

Angela paced around and checked her watch while Jack

spoke with his boss, the Special Agent in Charge. He held up his finger and mouthed "Just a second."

Jack ended the call and rejoined Angela on the sidewalk.

"Your boss?" Angela asked.

"Yeah. The SAC. He got a call from the Governor after my visit to the Hokanson's this morning. He wanted to know what I did to get the Governor's main contributor from Otter Tail County to call him."

"Wow," Angela said. "You OK?"

Jack smiled. "I told him that I handed the drug info off to you after trailing the delivery from the DL depot for Agent Kiley. I'm still on vacation. He told me to try and stay away from the Hokansons."

"So what are you going to do now?" Angela asked.

After checking the time on his phone, he answered, "We have a few hours until we spring Cyrus from the hospital. I think I'll go get Julie and the kids and hike in the state park."

"Looking for gold?"

Jack smiled. "What gold? How about you?"

"Heading out to the ranch."

"Looking for drugs?"

Angela shook her head in return and smiled. "What drugs?"

"Good luck," Jack said. "Let me know if I can help."

CHAPTER TWENTY-FOUR

A light breeze blew, rustling the long grass growing along
the edge of the parking lot. Jack stood in front of the
car, looked out over a field in the state park and smiled. They
were going to have some family time. Just them. They hadn't
had much on vacation so far. He spread some suntan lotion
on his face and neck and held out the bottle, ready to squirt
out some suntan lotion for whoever needed it. "Who else
needs some?" he asked.

"You're learning," Julie said. She put on a straw floppy hat
and sunglasses.

"I'm teachable," Jack said and laughed.

Willy had Vince on a leash. They walked along the grass,
Vince checking out their new surroundings.

Lynn said, "We're good, Dad. We already put some on.
Where are we hiking?"

Jack wiped the excess suntan lotion on the grass and
unfolded the map of the park. It was a flimsy eleven by
seventeen sheet of paper printed by the state park.

Julie joined Jack and leaned in next to him. "Where'd you
get this?"

"Cyrus gave it to me. It shows hiking paths around the park. He made some notes on the different routes," Jack answered. "I thought we'd try and find the old Hokanson homestead Cyrus told us about in his story the other night around the fire and retrace the path his father ran."

"Solve another mystery?" Julie asked.

"What mystery?" Jack asked back.

Julie backhanded Jack's bicep with a soft tap. "The gold. Why else did you throw the metal detector in the car?"

"To look for your ring."

"Right," Julie said. "Grab your map and we'll get this expedition underway." She slapped Jack on the butt. "Lynn, you have the backpack?"

"Yes, Mom."

"Water, snacks and bug spray?"

Lynn shifted the pack on her back. "I have everything, Mom."

"OK. Let's go kids. We're looking for treasure. Follow the leader." Julie smiled at Jack. "That's you, mister."

Jack shouldered his backpack with the metal detector and small shovels in it. Then he circled his index finger in the air and then pointed to the other end of the parking lot. "Let's go." He led the way down the dirt path through the grass, that wound through a field and into the woods.

Willy ran with Vince to catch up and walk next to Jack. "Where're we going, Dad?"

"We're going to see if we can find the old farm Cyrus talked about the other night in his story."

"It's really here?"

Jack smiled at Willy. To have no cares in the world and the wonder he did. "That's what we're going to find out. The story sounded real when he told it."

Sunlight poked through gaps in the leaves and branches of the tree canopy, speckling the dirt path in splotches of light.

They rounded a curve that brought them to the top of a hill. The path curved down to the right and ran along the shore of a small lake. Jack pulled the map from his pocket and unfolded it. Everyone gathered around him. "We're here." He pointed on the map. "Cyrus' notes say the homestead is on the other side of this lake. It doesn't look like there's a path so we're going off-trail. Everyone should take a drink of water and maybe spray your legs with bug spray."

After taking a break and drinking water and spraying their legs, they were ready to go. Jack took the lead again. This time Lynn followed at his heels. "So, this is where Cyrus' mom grew up?"

"Yep," Jack said. "Her family farmed this area." He stopped and pointed to the open area of grass to their left. "See this area? It may have had trees at some time, but people who settled this area cleared land for planting crops. It was a lot of work. They probably picked this area because of this lake for water or fish, and maybe the hills gave them some protection from the weather in the winter."

"Is Cyrus going to be OK?" Lynn asked.

Jack put his arm around Lynn's shoulder. "He's a tough old guy. He had a little setback, but he's going to be OK. We're going to pick him up from the hospital on the way back to the cabin. You guys can tell him about our little adventure."

They continued around the lake. Ahead, a group of trees hid the remains of a few buildings, an old farm. Willy ran ahead with Vince. "We found it!"

Julie grabbed hold of Jack's hand and they followed Willy and Lynn to the buildings. There wasn't much left of them but a pile of rotten wood and stone foundations. When they got there, Jack stood among them and pictured what the place may have looked like back when Cyrus' mother lived there. A white farmhouse, a barn, and a shed were arranged close together.

The kids started poking around what was the barn.

"Be careful, kids," Julie called out. She joined Jack. "Can you imagine living here?"

He reached out, grabbed her hand and held it in hers. "We could try, but with our gardening skills, I don't think we'd last long."

Julie laughed, turned to Jack and gave him a big hug. "Maybe hiking and exploring is more our thing."

Jack squeezed Julie back and kissed her. "OK, kids. Let's go," he said. Lynn and Willy came over with Vince. "What do you think?" Jack asked.

"It's cool," Willy said.

"I can't believe Cyrus was here as a kid," Lynn added.

"It's hard to believe," Jack said. "This is where the story started. The one he told us the other night around the fire. Do you remember what he said?"

Willy held out the dog tag hanging from his neck. "A guy was chased by some guys and dogs."

Lynn studied the house and the surroundings. "He said he heard them coming home and then they chased him."

Jack pointed to a break in the trees. "I bet that used to be a road into the farm. So, if they were coming from there and we know he ran towards the beach, where did he go?"

Julie added, "And where along the way did he possibly get rid of a bag filled with gold?"

The four of them gazed away from the farm towards the direction of the unseen beach.

"With the lake there, I think he had to go the way we came in," Willy said.

"Lead the way," Jack said.

WILLY AND VINCE broke through some bushes into a clearing. Jack, Julie and Lynn followed. They were about fifty yards east of the state park swimming beach. "Finally," Julie said.

Jack smiled and put an arm around Julie's shoulders. They were all sweaty and dirty. Exposed skin was red and scratched from pushing through the brush. "That was quite a hike, guys. Check your legs for ticks."

"What?" Lynn screamed.

"Just check your legs and make sure you don't have any ticks crawling on you. We've walked through a lot of fields."

Lynn started twisting and turning, trying to look at all sides of her legs. "Mom, will you check my legs?"

Jack started walking for the beach. "Let's go find a place to sit, rest and drink some water."

Willy stood on the shore. Vince strained at the end of his leash, trying to get to the lake.

"Willy, you coming?" Jack asked.

"Sure, Dad."

"What's up?"

Willy pulled on the leash to get Vince to follow. "I was just thinking about Cyrus' story." He fingered the dog license hanging from the string around his neck. "About the guy fighting with the dog here in the lake." He stared out at the water and then turned to face Jack. "Do you believe his stories?"

Jack ruffled Willy's hair. "Stories start from some fragment of the truth. And they change and grow as they're repeated from one person to the next. There's something true in his stories."

Lynn grabbed Jack's hand as they walked to a picnic table. "That was kind of a bust, Dad."

"You didn't like the hike?" Jack asked.

"We didn't find any sign of the gold."

"That's part of being an investigator. You learn from what

doesn't work. Now we know where not to look so we can focus somewhere else. You know what Cyrus told me?"

"What," Lynn asked.

"The gold will be in the last place you look. Think about it."

The four of them sat at a picnic table. Lynn emptied the backpack, placing bottles of water and snacks in the middle of the table. After eating a protein bar and a big drink of water, Jack refocused the family. "If Cyrus' dad did steal the gold and took it from the farm, where did he stash it? And is it still there?" Jack paused. "According to the story he swam from the island to the west side of the lake to get away from the brothers."

Lynn interrupted, "Cyrus didn't say he had the gold when the dog attacked him in the lake."

"Good point," Jack said. "But, all facts aren't in stories. For example, that story was about how the dog license may have ended up in the lake and Cyrus wasn't sharing his knowledge of the gold with us yet."

Julie added, "The man couldn't have carried the gold with him as he swam across the lake. It would be too heavy. He had to hide it somewhere or use something to float it across so he didn't sink."

"And if he did stash it, he may have told Cyrus' mother where it was for her to recover." Jack turned and looked down the beach towards the island. "We need to search from here to the island and we need to talk to Cyrus." Jack reached across the table and grabbed Julie's hand and rubbed her naked wedding finger. "And we need to get back here when the swimming area isn't so busy and find your ring." Julie smiled at Jack and squeezed his hand.

"Should we pack up and continue the hunt?" Julie asked.

Jack checked the time. "Maybe a quick search. We need to pick up Cyrus soon."

Lynn hoisted the backpack onto her shoulders again. "I think I figured it out, Dad."

"What?"

"The riddle. It will be in the last place you look. Because once you find it you won't be looking anymore."

Jack laughed. "That's right. Good job."

"OK," Jack said. "Cyrus' dad defeated the dog and has to get going. The brothers and the other dogs are coming." He looked back in the direction they came from. "He doesn't have a lot of time. If he had the gold in a bag, he picks it up. If it's in his pockets, he's weighed down and has to get going. I think he just runs for the island."

"Let's go," Willy said. He and Vince led the way.

They hiked across the grass and gravel, walking around the sunbathers on towels. Jack's phone rang. He checked it. "Hold up guys. Chief Angela is calling." He stepped away from the group and answered the phone.

"Hey, Chief. What's up?"

"Call me Angela, Jack."

Jack didn't say anything.

Angela continued, "We have a couple more OD's. Two dead, one on the way to the hospital."

Jack glanced at the kids. He wanted to swear. "I'm sorry," he said into the phone. "Where are you?"

"I'm on my way to the hospital to talk to the survivor to see if I can get some details."

Jack caught Julie's eye. She shot him a questioning look. He said into the phone, "let's meet at the hospital. We're at the State Park hiking. Give us thirty minutes."

He hung up and said to his family, "We'll search the island later, guys. Chief Angela needs to talk to me, so I told her we'd meet her in at the hospital since we have to pick up Cyrus." Nobody looked too disappointed. They were all tired and didn't believe they'd find any gold. They'd done enough hiking for today. "Now, let's see if we can find the car."

CHAPTER TWENTY-FIVE

The door to the hospital room was open. Jack and his family stopped and stood in the hallway, just out of Cyrus' view. The kids peeked into the room. Jack squeezed Julie's hand. She squeezed his back. They'd all grown to like the old guy over the last few days. He was almost like a grandpa to the kids. "He's OK," Jack whispered into Julie's ear. Cyrus was like a cat with multiple lives. They just didn't know how many he had left.

Jack knocked on the doorframe.

"Come in," Cyrus called out in a raspy voice.

Jack followed Julie and the kids into the room.

Cyrus sat in bed, tilted up so he could watch the television. The curtains were open and sunlight streamed into the room. "Hi guys," Cyrus said. "I thought you were my nurse."

The kids rushed to either side of the bed. "Dad said you can check out," Lynn said.

"Do you feel good enough to go fishing?" Willy asked.

"Whoa, kids," Julie said. She smiled at Cyrus. "Ready to get out of here?"

Cyrus nodded and added, "I'm a little tired, but I'm ready to leave."

"The doctor says you can leave if you come home with us," Julie said.

Cyrus scratched his temple and closed his eyes. "Hmm. I don't know."

"Come home with us," Lynn said, and she grabbed his hand.

"I hate to be a burden on your parents."

"We can help take care of you," Lynn said.

"We insist," Julie said. "Unless you'd rather stay here with the nurses."

Cyrus shook his head. "The nurses are nice, but the food's not so good. I thought I might just have to break out on my own."

Jack stepped forward and put his hands on Willy's shoulders. "I've got to talk to the Chief before we leave. Why don't you guys go to the park with Mom? I'll talk to the nurses and let you know when we're ready to go."

Cyrus brought Lynn's hand up to his lips and kissed her fist. He winked at Willy. "See you guys soon."

Julie left the room with the kids. Jack stood at the foot of Cyrus' bed and pulled out his phone. He sent a text to Angela to meet him in Cyrus' room. "You sure you're ready to go?" he asked Cyrus.

Cyrus cleared his throat and reached out for the white Styrofoam cup. He sipped water from the straw before answering. "I'm ready. Doc says I need to take it easy, says I need to quit smoking the cigars."

"Is that going to happen?" Jack asked.

Shaking his head, Cyrus said, "I don't think so. I'd light one up right now if I could."

"You'll be out of here soon enough, but you probably

don't want to light one up in front of Julie. She might kill you on the spot."

Cyrus chuckled and then broke into a coughing fit. He grabbed the water and took a sip.

There was a rap at the door. Jack turned, expecting to see a nurse, but it was Angela. "Hey, Chief," he said.

Angela gave him a nod in return, stepped in and closed the door to the room. She stood at the foot of the bed next to Jack. "You OK, Cyrus?"

"Yep. They cleared me to leave today."

"If he comes home with us," Jack added.

Cyrus used the bed remote to tilt the bed a little higher into a sitting position. "You aren't here just to check on me. Jack said you had to talk with him."

"They had some more OD's today," Jack said.

"What?" Cyrus exclaimed. "Damn it. What's going on?"

"That's what I want to know," Angela said. "It's been a growing problem the last couple of years, but it's accelerated now. And with the OD's the other night at the street dance and now these, today," Angela put her hands on her hips and looked at Jack. "I need some help."

Jack grabbed a couple of chairs that were along the wall for visitors and set them next to the bed. "Let's talk this through."

Angela plopped down in a chair and exhaled loudly.

"You're tired," Cyrus said.

"It's been a busy summer." She blew some hair out of her face. "Summer's always busy here with all of the lake people coming to their cabins. But, this one is worse. The street dance and the upcoming music festival are keeping us busy and the drugs are getting worse." Angela looked out the window and then continued, "We get some drunken drivers, parties, disturbances, but now the OD's. I'm pissed and worried. I dread the festival coming up. Whatever drugs are out there now are taking these young people out and we could have a tidal wave hit us at the festival."

Jack had been quiet. "You think it's just Clint and the Hokansons with the drug pipeline into the county?"

"Yes," Angela replied. "It can't be anyone else. The Hokansons wouldn't let that happen or I'd see some other sort of fallout from a turf battle."

Cyrus added, "And we know Clint's hauled drugs from the train in Detroit Lakes to the ranch."

"You get any of the people who sold these kids the drugs?" Jack asked.

Angela frowned and shook her head. "The survivors have kept quiet. They either don't know or they're too scared to cooperate."

"Well, we don't want the dealers," Jack said. "But, it would be nice if we could get a dealer to tell us who supplied them." Jack stood up and walked over to the window. Chicago, Minneapolis, the Dakota oil country, The Indian reservations, or Otter Tail County lake country, drugs caused problems everywhere. And it started with the greedy bastards who didn't care who got hurt as long as they made their money.

Jack turned back to Cyrus and Angela. "I think it's time we visited the ranch and reviewed layout, logistics, and security to prepare for the festival."

"That'll work," Angela said. "We're supposed to have a law enforcement planning meeting tomorrow. I can explain that you're offering your experience and need to see the ranch before the meeting."

"And snoop around to see if we can find some drugs," Cyrus said.

Jack tapped his nose and pointed at Cyrus. "Your brain's working. Maybe you are ready to get out of here," he said.

"But, you're rehabbing at the lake with Julie and the kids. The Chief and I will check out the ranch."

Cyrus threw back the sheets. "Get me my clothes and get me out of here."

"Hang on," Jack said. "I'll get the nurse to discharge you and get Julie and the kids back here." He shot a look at Angela. "Pick me up at the cabin?"

"I'll be there in an hour," Angela answered.

CHAPTER TWENTY-SIX

Angela turned off the county highway onto the ranch's gravel drive. A sign facing the main road announced the upcoming music festival. Trucks and trailers were spread out across the grounds. Workers were erecting booths and tents along with a big stage at one end of the outdoor rodeo arena. Music played over speakers. This was going to be a party.

"Cyrus wasn't happy we left him back at the cabin with your family," Angela said.

"Nope," Jack responded. "But, he's not strong enough physically or mentally to be out and about. He's got such a big chip on his shoulder for the Hokansons I was afraid he'd make things worse if we ran into any of them out here."

The gravel drive reached the main gates onto the grounds. A couple of private security people motioned for Angela to stop. She lowered the window and held out her credentials. "Chief Rancone, Pelican Rapids Police Department, I'm here to review some security measures."

The security officer took her credentials and studied

them. "I thought the security meeting with local law enforcement was the day after tomorrow," he said.

"We're here to see the layout, check out a few things and be prepared for the meeting," Angela answered.

"And you are?" the security officer asked Jack.

Jack had changed into jeans, boots, a polo shirt, baseball hat, and dark sunglasses. He didn't want to look like a lake bum and didn't know what he and Angela would run into searching the ranch. This was it: they were either getting through or getting turned away. "Jack Miller. I'm consulting on security with the Chief. Not only here, but also in Pelican Rapids." He handed his driver's license to the security officer.

After writing their info down on a clipboard, the security officer handed their identification back.

"Clint knows we're here," Angela said. She flashed him a smile. "He asked us to come out."

The security officer nodded to his partner to open the gate and let them pass.

"Thanks," Angela said. "Keep up the good work."

She pulled ahead and rolled forward slowly. "You didn't want to tell them you're with the FBI?"

"People get weird when they learn you're with the FBI. Things get serious, or they ask too many questions. I thought security consultant was good enough for now."

"Where do you want to start?" Angela asked.

"Let's start with the barns. Has to be somewhere big enough to store the drugs and keep them safe, out of the elements." Jack checked the time. "And let's be quick. We don't know how long we have. They might have called the Hokansons to tell them we're here." Jack pointed to a group of trucks parked at the end of the rodeo arena. "Let's park there and go on foot. If security comes looking for us, they'll find the truck but won't know where we are."

They got out of Angela's vehicle and walked towards the

barns. "Glad you didn't wear your uniform," Jack said. "A little less conspicuous dressed in jeans today." Scanning the grounds, Jack saw all the workers in jeans, t-shirts, work boots. Everyone was working hard.

"If you were going to hide a bunch of drugs, where would you keep them?" Jack asked.

Walking across the grass towards the three large white barns, Angela answered, "Someplace secure. A place with limited access. Makes me wonder if they're here since it's so busy."

"Might be just the place to be, surrounded by activity, but secure. You saw him drive here the other night after the Amtrak drop. Do you think they process and package them here too?" Jack asked.

"I guess we'll find out," Angela said. "They might buy it already packaged."

"Doesn't seem how they'd operate," Jack said. "Cuts into the profit margin letting someone else package it up for distribution."

They approached the three barns: large white buildings with green trim and matching green metal roofs. It was quiet around them. The doors were closed. No activity. "Which one?" Jack asked.

"Let's work left to right," Angela said.

The barn on the left had a service door to the right of the large, closed machinery entrance doors. Jack tried the knob. It turned. "It's open so they're probably not here, but let's check it out."

He looked back over his shoulder. No one seemed to be watching them. He pushed on the door and it swung open. He stepped in, quickly followed by Angela. They were in a large, open area. Light streamed in through windows that ran along the eaves. Jack pushed the door shut. "With it so open we should be able to check this place out pretty quick."

There was a cement floor, swept clean. "Looks like slab on grade, no basement." A couple of tractors were parked near the door with an old rusty Suburban next to them.

"Looks like we found the tractor barn," Angela said. "I think they use these for dragging the arena ground smooth and delivering hay to animals."

"Smells like a farm field," Jack said.

Angela was scanning above. "It's open up above. No loft."

Jack checked out the Suburban. It was empty. He nodded towards the far end. "Let's check out the office down there."

The office was locked, but they looked through a window facing the open floor of the barn. It looked like an office; a desk, some filing cabinets and shelves. Nothing else. Jack couldn't let a locked door go. He found a pile of scrap lumber by the tractors and grabbed a two-by-four that was about three feet long and walked back to the locked door.

"What's that for?" Angela asked.

"I'm going to try and pop the lock. With all of the hammering out there and the music blaring I don't think anyone will notice."

"Just a second." Angela stepped over to the closest window and looked out. She gave Jack a thumbs-up.

Jack positioned himself along the wall parallel to the door and stood like a batter at home plate. He swung the two-by-four and tried to hit the doorknob with the wide, open face of the board. He struck the knob and a stinging vibration transferred into his hands. "Ouch," he said and dropped the board. He shook his hands out.

"Get down," Angela hissed.

An ATV drove by the barn, passing by the window. By the sound of it, Jack could tell it kept going on its way. He tried the knob. It was still locked. He glanced over at Angela, shook his head and held up a finger. "One more try," he said quietly.

He picked up the board and positioned himself for another try. He rotated the board in his hands to hit the knob with the narrow side of the board this time. He imagined the pitch, eye on the prize, he thought and swung. The board bounded off the knob and rebounded out of his hands. His hands went numb and Jack sucked in a breath. He reached for the knob, but his hands wouldn't close.

Jack nodded for Angela to come over. She glanced out the window and then joined Jack. "My hands are all tingly, "Jack said. "See if it worked that time."

Angela grabbed the knob. It turned and she opened the door to the office.

They searched the desk drawers, the file cabinet, and the bookshelves. Jack scanned some papers on the desk for information, tried to log on to the computer.

Angela said, "Clint doesn't seem like a computer kind of guy. That's more Hanna's territory."

"You're probably right," Jack replied.

"Nothing here," Angela said. "Barn number two?"

THEY CROSSED the gravel and grass area between the buildings. Approaching the second barn, they heard some noises inside. Jack tried the door and found it open like the first. "Let's go," he said.

They stepped inside. This was the horse barn. Stalls lined the wall. Horses hung their heads out the openings above half doors of a few of them. A few more popped their heads out to see what was going on. Horse hooves scraped and tapped on the floor as the horses became agitated with newcomers coming into the barn.

"What do you think?" Jack asked.

"I don't even think it's worth searching unless one of the stalls is closed up and locked."

"Let's check them quick," Jack said. "I'll go left, you go right."

Jack walked down the center aisle with stalls on either side. He pet a couple of horses' noses as he walked by. There was an empty stall. He stuck his head in through the door. Hay covered the floor. A bridle hung on the wall. He checked the walls for openings. The floor was concrete. He exited and walked to the end and turned back to meet Angela at the center of the barn.

They had one barn left. They'd need some new ideas if that was a bust. "Anything?" he asked Angela.

She shook her head. "Some nice horses."

"You ride?" Jack asked.

"Just pony rides as a kid," Angela answered. "I was always kind of afraid of them."

"Let's go," Jack said. "One left."

They crossed to the third barn and checked the first service door they came to. The door was locked. Jack thought they might be on to something. "Let's go find another door," he said to Angela. They went around the corner to the front of the barn facing the arena and main area of the ranch. The security guard from the gate was on an all-terrain vehicle, headed straight for them.

Jack tried to talk to Angela without making it obvious. "Go check the next door. I'll talk to security when he gets here."

Angela passed by Jack and tried the lever on the larger barn door. "It's locked," she said.

The ATV pulled up next to them. "Wait a minute," the security officer said above the sound of the idling machine. "Mr. Hokanson..."

Jack interrupted him. "Did you know the other two barns are open? This one appears to be locked, but anyone could get into the other two barns. We'll need to talk to Mr.

Hokanson and tell him security leaves a little to be desired around here."

The security officer paused. He got a confused look on his face. "Mr. Hokanson wants me to escort you off of the property."

Jack held up his hand to stop the officer. "We'll be leaving after we check the doors on this building." He turned to Angela. "Finish checking the doors on this building, Chief." He turned his gaze back to the security officer. "We've got a job to finish here and then we'll leave."

The security officer sat on the idling ATV. Angela walked around the building checking all of the doors. She returned and reported to Jack, "the doors are all locked."

Jack smiled at the security officer. "One building's secure. You should check the others. We're leaving." Jack walked towards the parked cars. Angela followed.

When they got to Angela's vehicle, Jack whispered, "we need to get in that third barn."

CHAPTER TWENTY-SEVEN

"More overdoses?" Otto inhaled deeply through his nose and then blew the air out his mouth. Hanna sat across the desk from him.

"That's the word," Hanna said. "I think we need to face the facts." She paused. "Clint's effing this up. We need to forget about the drugs right now. We need to take a break. Let things cool down."

Otto leaned forward, placed his palms on the top of his desk to calm his nerves. "What about the festival?"

"The festival goes on. We're set to net a nice profit from the ticket sales, alcohol, and food, and we can still use it to launder the money we have from this summer's drug sales and our other businesses. We just won't get the bump we were expecting with all of the attendees. But we can't afford to have a massive number of people dying and that being associated with the festival."

Otto knew Hanna was right, but he was hoping that Clint would grow the drug business and put them in a position to expand out from the county, maybe to the North Dakota oil fields. The numbers would've compounded, his empire would grow to something his family had never imagined. "Where's your brother?"

Hanna shrugged. "He's been out since early this morning. Hopefully, cleaning up his mess."

Otto jabbed at the phone on his desk, putting it on the speaker mode and dialed Clint's number. After a couple of rings, Clint answered. "Where are you?" Otto asked.

"I'm heading to the ranch. Gate security called me and told me Angela and her FBI buddy were out there doing a security inspection."

"They let them in unaccompanied?" Otto asked.

"Yes," Clint responded. "It was Angela and she told them we'd talked about her doing an inspection. At least they called me after they let them in."

"They need to find them and get them to leave," Otto said.

"They're looking for them."

"Are you alone?" Otto asked. He didn't want anyone overhearing their conversation.

"Just me in the van," Clint said.

Otto looked at Hanna and nodded. "Clint, listen up. Hanna and I've been talking. With the OD's and now this news about Angela and Agent Miller at the ranch, we're pausing the drug business."

"What?" Clint yelled. "We're stopping? We're supplied and ready to go! We can't stop now."

"We need to lay low," Otto said to the phone. "That's it for now. We'll reassess after the festival and after Agent Miller is gone. After things have cooled down." Otto waited for Clint to say something. All he could hear was the background noise of the van. "You hear me, Clint?"

"Yeah, I heard you."

"Now, you get Angela and Agent Miller off of the

property. Tell Angela to come back for the scheduled security meeting tomorrow." Otto paused again.

"That's the plan," Clint answered.

Otto stared at the phone. If Angela and Agent Miller had been looking around, they had some suspicions. "Can you get the drugs out of there?"

Hanna nodded, showing she agreed with him.

Clint answered, "They're secured, but I can get them out of there in a van. Where should I take them?"

Otto ticked through the options in his head: the log home business site, ship them out of the county, bury them, put them in a truck and keep them moving. Too risky to move. What if they lost the load?

"Dad? You there?" Clint asked.

Otto answered, "Just a second, I'm thinking."

He shifted his gaze to Hanna. "We can't afford to lose this money."

Hanna shook her head. "It's going to hurt not having any cash flowing in if we just sit on it."

Otto turned back to the phone and leaned on the desk. "Clint."

"I'm here,"

"Can you sell it?" Otto asked.

"You said we weren't selling it. I'm supposed to move it," Clint said.

"I mean the whole thing at once. Back in the Cities, Chicago or the Dakota oil fields? The reservations up north?"

"You mean to our competitors?"

"Yes," Otto said. "Before the festival. We won't make as much, but we get it out of here and don't take a total loss to cash flow sitting on it. And we launder the money with the rest."

"You sure?" Clint asked.

"Yes."

"I can make some calls," Clint said.

"OK," Otto said. "Get it out of there and then make some calls."

"Where am I taking it?"

"Angela's got suspicions about the ranch. They were looking for something but didn't find it. Otto paused. "You have someone you trust?"

"Yeah, I got somebody."

"Here's what you're going to do," Otto said. "Get a couple more drivers in Hokanson vans. One heads towards Fergus Falls in case Angela is watching. If she follows, let her. One driver heads to Pelican Rapids. Again, let them follow. One driver brings the stash here. And whoever drives that one can't be followed."

"You want to move them home?" Clint asked.

"Yes, here, where we can watch them. They won't think we're dumb enough to keep them here."

"Got it," Clint said.

"Get it done." Otto ended the call.

CHAPTER TWENTY-EIGHT

A security guard stood in the middle of the drive, hands on his hips, blocking their exit. A second stood off to the side of the drive with a clipboard. Angela stopped and lowered the window.

"Just get us out of here," Jack mumbled, smiling and trying not to move his lips.

The security officer with the clipboard bent over to look in the window. "We were looking for you. Clint wanted us to find you."

Angela smiled. "Here we are. The other guy on the ATV found us. I'll give Clint a call. See you later." Angela raised her window and shifted into drive. The guard at the window motioned for the guard standing in the road to let them through.

Jack looked back at the security gate as Angela turned left onto the highway. "They aren't too curious about us."

"They're just regular security," Angela said. "They work for Hokansons, but we're law enforcement. What do you want to do?"

Jack had been thinking it through since they left the

third, locked barn. "Clint knows we're out here, so he may come out. If he doesn't, I want to sneak back in and check it out. Slow down a little." He released his seat belt and put his hand on the door release. Ahead on the right side of the road was a small lake. The shore closest to them was filled with cattails.

"What are you doing?" Angela asked.

They were the only car on the road. "Don't go too far. I'll call you if Clint comes." Jack cracked open the door and looked at the road. The blacktop whizzed past. "Slow down a little more, I'm no stuntman."

Angela jabbed the brakes and slowed the car some more.

"Wish me luck. I'll be hanging out in the cattails." Jack rolled out of the car and hit the road. He brought his hands up to protect his head. He kept rolling, so he didn't skid across the blacktop and rip the skin from his back. He rolled across the shoulder and into the ditch where he stopped, face down in the dry grass.

He lay still and blinked. The smell of dirt and weeds filled his nostrils. He moved his legs. They seemed OK. He stretched his arms out above his head and wiggled his fingers. Everything worked. He was too old for this. He heard the hammering from the work back at the ranch and crickets or grasshoppers in the grass. He raised his head and saw Angela driving away.

He army crawled on his stomach, elbows and knees, through the grass towards the lake, staying low to the ground. At the edge of the ditch, he reached a barbed-wire fence. He squeezed under the bottom strand of wire and crawled into the cattails.

The ground was damp. He felt his forearms and elbows and the fronts of his legs getting wet. A few feet into the cattails, Jack turned. He wasn't close enough to the ranch to get a good view of the entrance. He raised into a crouch and moved further into the cattails, then he turned and traveled parallel to the road, back to a position where he'd have a better view of the ranch.

He settled in on his stomach to watch the ranch. After a couple of minutes, his cell phone vibrated in his pocket. He pulled it out and answered it. "Angela," was all he said.

"Are you OK, Jack?"

Jack replied, "Maybe a little scraped up and wet, but I'll be OK."

"I'm in the parking lot of The Schoolhouse Bar. Clint just drove by in a Hokanson van. I'm thinking he's coming your way."

"I'll wait for him. Maybe you should head this way and wait a little closer."

"Be careful, Jack."

"You too," Jack answered.

A few minutes later, Jack watched as a white panel van with the Hokanson emblem on the side slowed and turned in to the ranch. That didn't take long. The sun reflected off the windshield and windows so he couldn't see who was driving. He assumed it was Clint, and it showed the Hokansons were worried and that there was something here on the ranch. Probably in the locked third barn.

Jack pulled his phone from his pocket and dialed Angela's number. "He's here," Jack said. "I couldn't see who was driving, but I assume it was Clint."

"You want me to come back? We can go into the ranch and go find him."

"No," Jack said. "They'd just delay our entry while they warned Clint we were there, giving him time to hide the drugs or whatever it is." Jack watched the van drive into the ranch, but lost sight of it. "And we don't have a warrant. I'm assuming since he came in the van and not on his bike that he's here to move something."

"I can just pull him over when he leaves," Angela said.

"That gets us Clint and the drugs, if he has them, but not the family. I think you have to try and follow him. See where he goes."

"Hey," Angela said. "Two more identical Hokanson vans just passed me."

"OK," Jack said. He put himself in Otto's place, trying to figure out what he was thinking. He knew that he and Angela had been at the ranch. Three vans. They couldn't have enough drugs that they needed three vans. It was a shell game. They were either splitting the load to minimize losses or making it harder to find the van with the cargo.

The two vans slowed on the road and turned into the ranch drive. "They're here," Jack said.

"What do you want me to do?" Angela asked.

"Hang on. I'll call you when the first van leaves. Follow him and see where he goes."

"What about the other two? You want me to just leave you there?"

"I think I have a plan," Jack said.

JACK CHECKED HIS WATCH. He didn't know how long he was going to be laying in the cattails or when he'd be back at the lake with his family. He thought he'd better check in with Julie, since he hadn't spoken with her all afternoon. Hitting favorites on his cell phone, he called her listening to the ring while he watched the ranch.

The call rolled over to Julie's voicemail. He'd never tire of her voice. "Hey, Jules. Sorry I haven't checked in for a while. Angela and I are still on this. I'll be back when I can. Love you." He had to get this drug business over with and get back to vacation, or Julie might leave him again.

A van rolled up to the exit at the ranch. Jack dialed

Angela. "They're coming out. You have the first one," he said. "Stay in touch."

"I wish I knew what you were doing," Angela said.

Jack exhaled a quick laugh. "I'll let you know when I know."

"Stay safe. This isn't your fight," Angela said.

"You too."

Jack watched as the first van turned and drove down the county highway. The other two vans rolled up to the exit. Jack rose from his prone position, grunted as he stretched his legs and pushed forward through the cattails. The second van exited the ranch and sped away. Jack reached the barbed-wire fence. The third van rolled up to security guards at the ranch exit. Jack pushed down on the top strand of fence wire and swung one leg over it.

He had to get out on the road to stop the third van. He thought if it didn't stop it contained drugs. If he could get it to stop, maybe he had a ride. As he swung his other leg over the fence, a barb snagged his pants leg. "Oh, come on," he said to no one. He pulled with his leg. It was connected to the fence by the barb.

He turned and watched the second van continue down the road. Swinging his gaze back to the exit, he saw the third van start to roll forward. Jack pushed off the ground with his free leg and dove towards the ditch. Prone in the air, his other leg was still stuck to a barb. Crashing to the ground, he jerked his leg and heard a tearing sound. He yanked again and his leg was free.

The third van turned onto the highway. Jack pushed himself up from the ground and ran across the ditch and then across the gravel and the weedy shoulder. Instinctively, he pulled his credentials from his rear pocket and flipped them open. Standing on the crown of the highway, he faced the oncoming van, holding his credentials out in front of him like a shield. "Stop, FBI," he commanded. The van stopped, its tires sliding on the hot pavement.

Jack hurried to the driver's door and swung it open. Van Halen music filled the air.

"What's up, man? Are you crazy?" the driver yelled. He was a young guy, maybe early twenties. Looked a lot like Clint, skinny, a scraggly beard.

"FBI. Where's your phone?" Jack asked. He didn't want the driver warning the others.

The driver glanced at the center console.

"Get out," Jack commanded. "Hurry."

The driver fumbled with the seat belt, unbuckled it and got out of the van. Jack grabbed him by the back of the neck, walked him to the rear of the van and opened the door. He gave him a push. "Get in."

Jack slammed the door and hurried to the driver's door. He hoped security was busy and not watching the vans after they left. He glanced up ahead. The second van was visible climbing a hill. He jumped into the driver's seat and accelerated to keep the van ahead of him in sight.

CHAPTER TWENTY-NINE

Jack saw brake lights from the van ahead of him light up as the driver slowed, stopped and turned left to head north at the highway intersection. It helped him that the other driver was obeying traffic laws.

Jack could hardly think with the music blaring so loud. He found the volume and turned it down until it was silent.

"Where were you going?" Jack said to the guy he'd placed in the back of the van. They were separated by steel mesh between the front seats and the back end. The back end was empty except for the guy sitting on the floor. The drugs had to be in the van ahead of them.

"Nowhere, man," the guy said. "Can you just let me go? Why are you keeping me back here?"

"There were three vans," Jack said. "Hang on." He tapped the brakes and slowed at the intersection and took the turn without stopping. Jack heard the guy in the back fall into the wall of the van and then back into the middle as he struggled to maintain control of the van through the turn.

"Shit, man. I'm gonna get hurt back here. Be careful."

Jack accelerated to decrease the distance between him

and the second van. The guy fell onto his back. The road ahead was full of turns and Jack didn't want to lose him if he turned off the highway.

"There are three vans," Jack repeated. "Where are you all going?"

The guy in the back stayed silent.

"Let me know where you're all supposed to go and I'll stop and let you out." Jack checked his speed. He sped up to seventy-five on a straight stretch of road. Ahead there was an area with a few homes along the road and the posted speed limit was forty. Jack could make up some ground on the second van there.

"What did Clint tell you?" Jack asked.

"You'll let me go?" the guy asked.

"If you tell me what's going on, I'll let you go."

The guy had crawled up to the cage and grabbed onto the wire mesh. "Man, I don't know. Clint would kill me."

Jack glanced in the rearview mirror and met the guy's eyes. "Help me bust him and he can't hurt you. Don't help me and I'll bust you as aiding in drug distribution."

"You really FBI?" the guy asked.

Jack held his credentials up, facing the rear of the van. "Yes, I'm really FBI."

The guy peered through the mesh. "OK. Clint called us and told us to get to the ranch. Me and Tom. He's driving that van."

"And? You put something in one of the vans?" Jack asked.

"A couple of big coolers. They're strapped down in the back of Tom's van. That one up there." The guy pointed a finger through the mesh.

"Where's he going?" Jack asked.

"Back to the Hokansons."

Jack glanced into the rearview mirror. "Straight to Hokansons?"

"Depends if he thought he was being followed or not."

Jack backed off on the accelerator. Now he knew where to go. He didn't need to follow so closely.

"Where were you supposed to go?"

"I was just supposed to take an easy drive to Pelican, visit a few places like the high school, the hardware store, the park."

"OK," Jack said. "How about Clint?"

"Clint?" the guy asked.

"In the first van," Jack answered.

"Umm, Clint wasn't in the first van. Victor's driving that one."

Jack turned his head back to look at the guy in the back. Clint wasn't in the first van? This info threw Jack for a second. He needed to refocus. He'd figure this out.

"To where?"

"Fergus Falls beer distributor."

"The van's empty?" Jack asked.

"Yep."

"Alright. If he's not in the first van, where's Clint?"

"We left him at the ranch."

"What?" Jack said. He kept driving down the highway. Now, what was he going to do?

"Clint drove out to the ranch with Victor, but after we loaded up the van and he told us what to do, he stayed behind. You going to let me go?" the guy in the back asked.

"Hold on," Jack said. He called Angela on his cell phone.

"Jack, looks like ... to Fergus Falls," Angela said when she answered. Her call was breaking up.

"Head on back," Jack said. "The van's empty and Clint's not driving that one."

"What?" Angela asked. "I can't ... very well. These hills ... it hard to ... you."

Jack or Angela's signal was getting blocked.

Jack spoke a little louder and enunciated his words. "I'll explain. See you at our cabin."

"Your cab... in twenty min...," Angela replied.

THE BOAT LANDING WAS BUSY. Most of the open space was taken up by trucks and boat trailers left in the gravel parking lot by people out fishing or boating on the lake. Jack pulled off the highway into the gravel lot and parked.

"You going to let me go?" the guy asked.

"Just a minute." Jack made another call. "Julie, can you load the kids up in the boat and come and pick me up at the boat launch?"

"Everything OK?" she asked.

"Yeah. Angela and I split up, so I need a ride. It's faster if you come by boat."

"I'll just let Cyrus rest. I'll find the kids and we'll be on our way."

"OK, see you soon," he said, and ended the call.

Jack got out of the van. He could keep an eye on the Hokanson's driveway from here. He let the second van go on its meandering drive without him since he knew where it was going, right back here after a little drive.

It had been a long day and it was catching up with him. He stretched his arms and yawned.

The guy in the van hammered on the sides. "You going to let me out of here?"

Jack opened the back. "Before you get out, show me some ID."

The guy took his wallet out of his pocket and pulled out his driver's license.

Jack took it and took a picture of it with his cell phone. "Thanks, Alan." He handed his ID back to him. "You're free to go. Now get out of here. I think it best if you just go home. Don't talk to anybody." He held up his phone with the picture of Alan's ID. "I know who you are and where to find you."

"Yeah, man. I got it." Alan jumped into the van. The tires spun and spit gravel as he drove away.

Jack checked the time. No wonder he was hungry. It was suppertime and he hadn't eaten all day. He leaned against the one tree at the boat launch to stay out of the sun and not be too obvious while he watched the entrance to the Hokansons.

Jack thought about what he had learned from Alan, that Clint had stayed at the ranch. He and Angela needed to figure this out before he could rest.

He spied a van driving back across Stony Bar. It slowed and turned into the Hokanson drive. So, the drugs were probably here in a couple of coolers. What did he and Angela start by visiting the ranch?

Jack heard a boat coming towards the boat launch. He walked out onto the dock and waited. Willy waved at him. Jack waved back. Julie cut the power to the boat and its momentum carried it towards the dock.

"Hi, Dad!" Lynn called.

Jack bent over and caught the boat as it glided in and stopped it next to the dock. "Nice job, Julie. Not bad for a new boater."

"I'm getting the hang of it," she said.

Jack pushed the boat away from the dock and jumped in. "I'm hungry. You guys make anything for supper?"

"We're having a fish supper," Willy answered. "Cyrus helped us clean some fish and told mom another way to cook them."

"Have enough for Chief Angela? She's meeting me back at the cabin." He winked at Julie. "OK, Captain. Let's go back. You're driving."

CHAPTER THIRTY

A nother beautiful sunset over Lake Lida. Otto sat on a bench on the shore by the dock, smoking a cigar. The people out on the lake in their boats or on their jet skis, soaking in as much fun as they could as August drew to a close, wouldn't guess the pain and turmoil the Hokanson family was feeling tonight.

Otto's dream of riches that he believed would come with growing into the drug baron of western Minnesota and the North Dakota oil basin was evaporating. Chief Rancone and Agent Miller had spoiled his plans.

He blew a cloud of smoke up into the air. He agreed with Hanna's plan of selling the drug supply for now, but it would be a stretch to break even and he was putting his faith in Clint's hands. Clint knew the drug business and the players, but he was more muscle than brains.

Sometimes he couldn't believe that both of his kids came from the same mother. Hanna had the brains, ambition and strategic mind that they needed to weather this storm and succeed in the future.

His cell phone buzzed in his pocket, but he ignored it.

The drugs had made it successfully from the ranch to the storage shed. The driver Clint trusted was good. He made the delivery no questions asked. Otto took another deep drag from his cigar. Maybe he should take the speedboat out for a spin and join the others out on the lake. He watched a pair of loons swimming a hundred yards offshore, diving for their supper.

The cell phone buzzed again. Otto pulled it from his pocket. It was Clint. Otto took the call. "Yes," was all he said.

"Dad, where are you?"

"Down by the lake. Thinking about going for a boat ride. Why?"

"Not over the phone. Come up to the house. Now." Clint said, and he ended the call.

Otto was surprised. Clint was rarely so direct with him. He got up from the bench, threw his cigar into the lake and headed for the house.

CLINT PACED BACK and forth next to a rusted Suburban parked in the driveway. He was sucking hard on a cigarette. He held an unlit cigarette in his other hand.

"Whose truck is this?" Otto asked.

"I bought it cheap for cash so I could drive around unnoticed for a while."

"OK. What was so urgent you needed to see me?"

Clint threw the stub of the cigarette he was smoking on the ground, lit the fresh one and took a huge drag from it. He nodded towards the back of the Suburban. "Back here."

They walked to the rear of the Suburban and Clint opened the rear doors. "This," was all he said.

"Damn it, Clint," Otto said. "Is he alive?"

Cyrus lay in the back of the truck. Face up, his eyes were

closed, blood at the corner of his mouth and on his chin, wrists bound together over his stomach.

"Yeah, he's alive."

Otto ran through the options in his head. He closed the truck doors. "Get in."

Clint walked towards the driver's side.

"Other side. I'm driving," Otto said.

"Don't you want to know what happened?" Clint asked.

"Yep, just hold on to it for a minute." Otto drove the Suburban down the drive to the barn. "Open the door," he said to Clint.

Otto parked the truck next to the van that Clint's driver had stashed here earlier. He met Clint at the back of the truck and opened the doors to keep an eye on Cyrus. Clint lit up another cigarette.

"OK, what happened?" Otto asked.

Clint locked eyes with Otto and then looked away. "I was pretty sure the Fed was watching the ranch with Angela, so I thought it might be a good time to go by the cabin to get Cyrus to talk about the gold."

"The gold?" Otto asked.

"Yeah. With what's going on with the drugs I know we're taking a financial hit so I thought we should take a crack at the gold." Clint glanced at Cyrus. "And with his health issues, I didn't think we had much more time. It was now or never. Grab him, get him to tell us where the gold is and we're set."

"And?"

"Cyrus was alone at the cabin."

Otto turned and stood next to Clint and studied Cyrus. "It looks like he's breathing. What happened?"

Cyrus coughed once, moved his head, and coughed again. "He hit me."

CHAPTER THIRTY-ONE

Julie drove the boat across the lake at full throttle. With the noise of the motor and the wind blowing, it was hard to talk, so Jack just enjoyed the ride with his family. "This is fun!" she yelled.

Jack and Willy sat in the two rear seats and faced the back of the boat. Willy hung his arm over the side of the boat and let his hand bounce on the water pushed up by the boat. Once in a while he'd flick the water from his hand at Jack or Lynn.

Lynn sat in the seat next to Julie and stood to raise herself above the windshield and let the wind blow her hair. She yelled into the wind.

This was how vacation was supposed to feel. Not a care in the world, having fun with your family. Jack smiled and howled into the sky with Lynn.

The boat slowed as they approached the cabin. Julie let it drift in idle as she turned the wheel to guide the boat next to the dock.

"You're pretty good at this," Jack said. He tied the rear

end to the dock, grabbed the front rope and jumped onto the dock to secure that to the dock, too.

"It's been a while, but my grandparents had a boat. My grandpa would let me drive once in a while."

"Can one of you pull us behind the boat on the tube later?" Willy asked.

"Sure," Julie answered. "But let's go get something to eat in the cabin and check on Cyrus."

Willy and Lynn jumped out of the boat onto the dock.

Julie shouted after them, "and make some lemonade. Chief Angela is stopping by."

Jack put out his hand and helped Julie step from the boat onto the dock. He wrapped her in his arms and hugged her. "Sorry I was gone all day," he said.

"Angela needs the help. It's awful what's happening to these young people around here," Julie said, her head resting against his chest. "You kind of smell."

"I was laying in cattails most of the afternoon."

"You didn't call Linda about the jobs, did you?"

"I was kind of busy."

"You have to call her, Jack."

A piercing scream came from the cabin. Jack turned his head.

"The kids," Julie said. She gave Jack a slight push on his chest. "Go."

"Dad!" Jack heard Lynn scream. He ran from the dock and up the grassy hill towards the cabin.

"Dad! Help him!"

Jack saw the kids back by the gravel road behind the cabin. They were kneeling over something. There was blood. He joined them and found they were attending to Vince, lying on the grass, panting. He whined quietly. His chest and side were bloody.

"What happened, Dad? Is he going to be OK?" Willy asked.

"Did he get hit by a car?" Lynn asked.

Jack placed his hand on Vince's head to comfort him. There was a lot of blood. He started feeling around the fur looking for the source.

Julie joined them. "Oh my God," she said.

Taking control of the situation, Jack started issuing orders. "Willy, go grab me a blanket and some of my t-shirts for rags. Lynn, go get me a pan of water from the kitchen sink." The kids ran to the cabin.

"What happened?" Julie asked.

Jack probed the fur some more and found the source of the blood. It wasn't a broken leg or rib poking through the skin. He looked up at Julie. "I think somebody shot him."

Julie's hand shot to cover her mouth. "Shot?" she said. "The kids. Where's Cyrus?" She turned and ran to the cabin.

Jack started to stand and follow Julie when he saw the kids coming from the cabin with the things he had sent them for. They were OK. Whoever did this must not be around, he thought. But where was Cyrus?

The kids carefully put their supplies on the ground next to Vince. "You guys kind of gently place your hands on his head and side to comfort him while I clean him up." Jack poured some of the water over where he thought the wound was and gently wiped the fur with a t-shirt. Vince panted and whined.

Julie came back from the cabin. Jack continued to work on Vince. Without looking up he said, "I'm going to take him to the vet in Pelican Rapids. I saw one across the road from the Dairy Queen. Can you call them and tell them I'm bringing him in?"

"Jack, Cyrus isn't inside," Julie said.

"Maybe he went somewhere," Jack said.

"He's gone. It looks like there's been a fight inside. There's stuff all over the place. And somebody did this to Vince."

Jack quit working on Vince. He didn't know what to do. He looked at Julie; her hands were behind her back. "We'll all go," Jack said.

"No," Julie said. Her hands came out from behind her back. She held out his holstered Glock. "You go. Get Vince to the vet and find Cyrus. I'll call Angela and tell her to meet you there."

Jack took the Glock and clipped the holster to his belt.

"What about you guys? I can't leave you here," Jack said.

Julie switched his snub-nosed revolver from her left to her right hand and it hung by her side. "I don't think they'll be back. But, if they do come back, I'll be ready. And you said Angela's on her way."

"OK," Jack said. He knew Julie could shoot either of his weapons: the Glock or the revolver. He'd taken her to the range many times. She'd hit what she was aiming at.

"Tell Angela I'll meet her here after I've got Vince settled with the vet," Jack said. "I'll feel better if you're both here."

He stepped over and gave Julie a hug and a kiss. Then he knelt by the kids and asked them to help move Vince onto the blanket. Vince panted and whimpered, but seemed to understand they were trying to help him.

Jack gave each of the kids a hug. "Listen to your mom," he said. "I love you guys." Then he carried Vince to the car, put him in the back seat and headed to town.

CHAPTER THIRTY-TWO

"He hit me and he shot the dog," Cyrus said.

"What?" Otto cried. He cuffed Clint on the back of the head. "What have you done? You shot their dog?"

Clint took a couple of steps away from Otto and rubbed the back of his head. "I was walking Cyrus to the truck and the dog came running from the lake. He surprised me. It was just a reaction."

"They aren't going to be happy he shot their dog," Cyrus said.

"Shut up," Clint said to Cyrus.

"And where's the dog?" Otto asked.

"I left him lying on the grass where he fell," Clint said.

"You should've grabbed him. Maybe they would have thought he'd run away. Now they have their family pet shot dead."

Otto pointed at Cyrus. He felt the rage building up inside. Now wasn't the time. "Just watch him," he said to Clint, and headed for the garage door.

"Where are you going?" Clint asked.

"I need to think," Otto said.

"I think you need to run," Cyrus said from the back of the truck.

"Shut up," Clint said.

Otto stood outside the garage, his back pressed up against the wall. He patted his pockets, looking for a cigar. They were empty. He closed his eyes and took measured breaths, inhaling slowly, holding it and then slowly exhaling.

He couldn't believe how everything had fallen apart so close to the finish line. What were they going to do? With Cyrus gone from Agent Miller's cabin and the dog shot after Miller and the Chief had been to the ranch, they'd come here soon. They couldn't stay. In a way, Cyrus was right. It was time to get out of here.

Otto stepped back into the garage. Clint paced at the back of the Suburban smoking, a cigarette. "Give me one of those," Otto said. He imitated smoking a cigarette, bringing his hand up to his lips.

Clint tapped one out of the pack, handed it to Otto and gave him his lighter.

Otto lit the cigarette and inhaled deeply. The smell of freshly lit cigarette tobacco was good. It brought back some memories of his younger years. He blew the smoke towards the ceiling of the garage. "Get some rope and tie Cyrus' hands together. Then we'll move the coolers from the van to the truck. Put them in the back with Cyrus." He took another drag from the cigarette. "Where's the gun?"

"What?" Clint asked.

"The gun you shot the dog with," Otto said.

"It's up in the front seat," Clint nodded towards the truck.

"Full clip?" Otto asked.

"Except for the two shots I took at the dog."

Otto threw what was left of his cigarette on the floor of

the garage and ground it out with the toe of his shoe. "OK, tie him up." He walked to the back of the truck to address Cyrus. "Behave. OK?"

"Hope you have a good plan," was Cyrus' answer.

Otto pulled his cell phone from his pocket and called Hanna. "Hey, you feeling good enough to go away with us for a couple of days?"

"Yes, I'm fine," Hanna answered.

"OK," Otto said. "Throw some food and water together. Enough for a day or two. And grab the pistols from my office and a couple of boxes of ammo. We'll pick you up at the front door in a few minutes. Call me if you see anyone coming up the drive."

Hanna didn't ask any questions. She just ended the call. Otto knew she'd be ready.

RAINDROPS SPECKLED THE WINDSHIELD. Otto slowed and drove the Suburban past the state park check-in gate. He knew it wasn't staffed after hours. It was the trust system now. He followed the narrow two-lane blacktop road as it curved through the park, up and down gentle hills.

"Where are we going?" Clint asked. He rode in the back seat behind Otto. To get the coolers and provisions into the back, they had to move Cyrus into the back seat. He sat quietly behind Hanna.

"After what you did tonight, we needed to leave home. They'll look for us on our properties," Otto said. He turned off the paved road onto a service road. "Hang on." The road was a couple of ruts through the grass. They bounced along the path, past a stand of trees and turned. Ahead was an old barn.

"It's still standing?" Cyrus asked.

"I get it fixed up and reinforced once in a while," Otto

said. "Clint, here. Take this." Otto handed a leather fob with a couple of keys attached to it over the seat. "Jump out and open the doors."

Clint got out of the Suburban and walked to the barn. Cyrus coughed in the back seat. He grunted, "you keeping it for sentimental reasons or what?"

"I've got a deal with the park. As long as it's standing, it's mine, and this little plot of land remains private property. Part of the deal when Dad turned over this farmland to the park."

Clint swung open the barn doors and Otto three-point turned, backing the truck inside.

"Dad, I have to pee," Hanna said.

Otto put his hand on Hanna's arm and smiled at her. "There's a portable toilet in the corner behind the curtain."

"It's kind of dark in here," Hanna said.

"The walls are lined with tar paper. I'll light a couple of lanterns so we have some light. Nobody should notice we're here from outside." Otto stepped out of the truck. He stuck his head back in and said to Cyrus, "sit tight until we get everything set." He grabbed the pistol Clint had left under the seat and went to unload the gear.

WATER DRIPPED FROM THE CEILING. Avoiding the water, they arranged three chairs in a semi-circle facing a lone chair. Cyrus sat in that chair. Clint had tied a rope from his ankle to the back of the chair. Otto sat in the chair facing him, with Clint and Hanna on either side. "Cyrus, why did you come back to Pelican Rapids? You're gone your entire adult life and then you show up." He pulled a cigar from his pocket, snipped the ends.

"Can I have one of those?" Cyrus asked.

Otto lit the one he'd prepped and handed it to Cyrus. Then he prepped and lit one for himself.

"This is nice compared to what I usually smoke," Cyrus said. He coughed and spit on the floor. "What are you going to do with me?"

CHAPTER THIRTY-THREE

Jack walked into the cabin and wiped the rain from his face.

"Dad's back!" Lynn yelled and ran to him. She threw her arms around his waist.

The lights were all on in the cabin. Julie and Angela sat at the table with coffee or tea in front of them. They were situated where they could see the road out of the window. Willy was on the floor, sorting through his fishing tackle box. They all turned to him.

"Is Vince going to be OK?" Lynn asked. Her emotion-filled face looked up at him.

Jack carefully peeled Lynn's arms from around his legs and held her hand. They walked to the table and sat down. Willy came over and climbed onto Jack's lap. "The vet says he thinks he'll be OK, but he'll need some recovery time. I wanted to get back here to you guys, but he'll call me if there are any updates."

"Can we see him?" Willy asked. "He'll be lonely."

Jack pushed Willy's hair back and kissed his forehead.

"We'll go see him tomorrow. Maybe you can pick out a toy or something to bring for him."

"What about Cyrus?" Lynn asked.

Jack put an arm around her shoulder and pulled her close. "We need to figure out what happened to him and bring him home."

"He's OK?" Willy asked.

"I'm sure he is," Jack said.

"Why don't you guys run upstairs and draw some pictures for Vince and the vet's office and we'll deliver them tomorrow," Julie said. "And some welcome home cards for Cyrus."

The kids ran up the stairs to the loft. The French press on the island was half full of coffee. Jack felt the glass. It was cool. He poured the coffee into a mug and put it in the microwave to warm it up.

"Vince is really going to be OK?" Julie asked.

Jack nodded. "Yep. We got lucky. He'll recover." Jack watched the mug circle around the inside of the microwave until it dinged. Jack grabbed his mug of coffee and joined the women at the table. It felt good to sit down. He felt the tension and fatigue in his limbs. His hand started to shake when he reached for the coffee. He shook both of his hands and flexed his fingers and took a deep breath and blew it out. "OK," he sighed. "Any news on Cyrus?"

"No," Julie said. "I assured the kids that he's OK, but we haven't heard anything."

Angela added, "it looks like he was probably taken."

"Agreed," Jack said.

Julie stuck out her hand. "Give me your phone."

Jack pulled his cell phone from his pocket. "It's just about dead. What do you need it for? Where's yours?"

"I'll explain," Julie said. She got up from the table and walked to the bedroom. She returned with a charging cord and plugged Jack's phone in to charge it. "When we left to pick you up at the boat landing, I gave my phone to Cyrus in case he needed to reach us or if we needed to call him."

"And he hasn't called," Jack said. "You've tried calling him?"

Julie shook her head. She handed Jack his phone. "Unlock it."

Jack entered the code to unlock the screen and handed it back to Julie. She scrolled thru the apps and opened the Find My Phone app.

"Angela and I have been talking. We decided to wait for you. We couldn't call him and give away that he has my phone if they haven't found it on him," Julie said.

"Assuming someone has him," Angela added. "If he was able to call us, he would've called by now."

Julie touched the screen to launch the app. "But, if there's cell service where he is, we should be able to see where is on the map." Julie set the phone on the table for them all to see.

Jack reached across the table, grabbed Julie's hand and squeezed it. "Beauty and brains. That's why I love you," he said.

Jack, Julie, and Angela all leaned forward and waited for the app to display a map showing where Julie's phone, and hopefully, Cyrus, were located. A map popped up. At the top it said "Julie's phone" and a symbol of the phone appeared in the heart of Maplewood State Park.

"I could kiss you," Jack said.

"Go ahead," Julie answered.

Jack leaned across the table and kissed her on the lips and sat back. A sense of relief further eased the tension in his arms and shoulders.

"X marks the spot," Angela said. "Now what?"

Jack pushed back from the table. "Assuming the old guy's alive, we're not going to just rush in. I'm going to make some fresh coffee. My phone is going to charge. We're going to watch and see if Cyrus moves. We're going to eat something. And we're going to make a plan."

It was weird not having Vince at their feet, waiting for something to drop as they prepared supper. Jack stood at the stove, browning hamburger and boiling water for spaghetti. Julie and Angela were at the island behind him, chopping vegetables for a salad and making garlic toast.

Jack heard the kids upstairs debating what to draw. At least they weren't fighting. "I got a hold of an agent in the Fargo office. He'll be here in a couple of hours. It's about an hour drive once he gets his stuff together. He'll come and keep an eye on you and the kids," Jack said to Julie. He turned to Angela. "You have a deputy we can trust?" he asked. "We don't know who we can trust in the Sheriff's office, right?"

Angela stopped chopping the onion. "I trust our admin with my life. Doris, you met her. And I have one of my three officers that I believe I can totally trust. Dane Larby. He's new, but I trust him. He grew up around here playing football. He knows the area and only wants to do what's best for Pelican and the county."

"Sounds good," Jack said. "Call him and have him meet us at your station in a little bit? Don't share too much, just in case. Just tell him to be dressed for an outdoor operation."

CHAPTER THIRTY-FOUR

Rain dripped from the ceiling of the barn and splashed in small puddles on the gravel floor. The wind gusted, blowing a mist of water in through the door. "Clint, close the door so we don't get blown out of here," Otto said.

Clint pulled the two barn doors shut and latched them to keep them from blowing open. The inside of the barn grew a little darker as the afternoon light got cut off from the entrance. The gas-fired lanterns hissed as they burned.

Otto sucked in on his cigar. The ember glowed red on the end. He blew the smoke towards the ceiling.

"I thought we weren't smoking around Hanna," Clint said.

"She's almost ready to give birth," Otto said. "A little smoke isn't going to hurt now. Right?" he directed his question at Hanna.

"I'm fine," she replied. "I might move over by the window if I feel nauseous.

"OK," Otto said. He leaned forward in his chair, resting his elbows on his knees and directed his gaze at Cyrus. "Cousin, what are you doing here?"

Cyrus returned Otto's stare. "Cousin," he spat out. "I'll

tell you what I'm doing here. My wife died. My health is failing. I decided to come back and see Otter Tail County again in the summer. The best time to be here."

"That's a nice promotional statement for the tourist bureau, but why are you here? Really. You've been nothing but a thorn in our side since you came to town, looking into our businesses, asking questions at the city offices, talking to a lawyer and now teaming up with this FBI agent."

Cyrus smiled. "I've been returning to my roots, enjoying the area, the sites of the state park. If it wasn't for your son here, I probably would've never even met Jack Miller and his family. It was your son who picked a fight with me and Jack intervened. Luckily for Clint."

"What?" Clint jumped up.

Cyrus didn't flinch. He held his gaze with Otto.

"Clint," Otto said to stop him. "Sit down. Don't let him get to you."

Clint huffed and sneered at Cyrus, stomped a foot on the floor and returned to his chair.

Otto continued, "I'm sure you heard the family stories over the years. Your mother shared them with you."

"What stories?" Cyrus asked. He sat back in his chair and took a puff from his cigar.

"Clint thinks you came back to look for the gold."

"The gold?" Cyrus asked.

"Yes, the gold," Otto said. "Your father, the man whose seed impregnated my aunt, stole a bag of gold and hid it. Now, you're back here poking around the park, the cemetery. You have a metal detector." Otto let it hang there.

Cyrus started coughing. A chest-deep cough causing him to curl forward. He put his free hand over his mouth. "Can I get some water?"

"Get him a bottle of water, Clint," Hanna said.

Otto watched him cough. He gauged his health, his ability to talk and answer his questions.

Clint grabbed a bottle of water from a case of water sitting in the back of the truck. He held it out for Cyrus on his way back to his chair. "Need me to open it for you, old man?" he asked.

Cyrus coughed again, grabbed the water from Clint. "Thanks. I got it." He set his cigar on the floor and twisted the cap from the bottle. After he took a big drink he stared at Otto, "I don't know anything about some lost gold." He chuckled. "That's why Clint grabbed me? That's why he shot an FBI agent's dog?" He laughed again. "You guys are screwed."

Otto gave it one last try. "Tell us where the gold is," he paused, "or where you think it is, and we'll split it with you." Otto studied Cyrus for a tell, a hint that he knew what he was talking about. Cyrus stared into his eyes and didn't flinch. Otto inhaled his cigar and blew the smoke out of the corner of his mouth towards Clint, away from Hanna.

Cyrus picked up his cigar, inhaled and blew the smoke directly at Otto and the other two.

Clint jumped up and charged Cyrus. "Damn it! Where's the gold!" he bellowed.

Cyrus didn't flinch. He just continued to stare at Cyrus. "Was there ever any gold, Otto? Or was it just a family story passed down over the years?"

"Clint, sit down," Otto said. He directed his attention back to Cyrus. "Well, I think you believe the story about the gold. It's why you're here." Cyrus was stubborn. Otto needed to calm things down. He decided he'd try again after a little break. Maybe when he was tired. Maybe with a little alcohol in his system. Or they had the drugs. "I think we should eat something and talk about what we're going to do next."

CHAPTER THIRTY-FIVE

Jack and Angela walked into the conference room at the Pelican Rapids police station. Doris had a fresh pot of coffee and bottles of water waiting for them on a counter at one end. "Let me grab my laptop," Angela said.

The beacon on Jack's cell phone showed Cyrus, or Julie's phone at least, was still in the same place in the state park. He poured a cup of coffee and moved the chairs from the conference table back to the walls. He wanted to make room for them to move around and he knew they wouldn't want to sit as the caffeine and adrenaline pumped into their systems.

A man stepped into the doorway and stopped. He wore camouflaged rain gear. Water dripped from his hat. He studied Jack. "You must be Dane," Jack said.

"Yes, sir."

Jack walked over and stuck out his hand. "I'm Jack Miller." Dane Larby grabbed Jack's hand, a solid grip.

"The Fed?"

Jack nodded, "Yep." Dane was a big guy. Not tall, maybe just over six feet, but he was solid. A good addition for tonight's operation. "The Chief will be back in a second. Come on in," Jack said. "Grab something to drink."

Dane took off his coat, hung it on a chair and grabbed a water. "What's going on tonight?"

"We'll wait for the Chief," Jack answered.

Lightning flashed and a couple of seconds later thunder made the windows rattle. "We're going out in this, right?" Dane asked.

Jack nodded and walked over to look out the window. The sun colored the clouds grey. It'd be getting darker.

Angela walked into the conference room carrying her laptop. "Hey, Dane. You guys met?"

"Yes, ma'am," Dane said.

Jack chuckled. "Yes, ma'am."

"Shut up, Jack." Angela plopped her laptop onto the conference table and opened it up. She connected to the big monitor on the wall and shared her screen. A satellite image of the state park came up.

"Think we should bring Dane up to speed?" Jack asked.

"Right," Angela said. She leaned forward, planted her hands on the table and stared at Dane. "The number and severity of drug overdoses have been growing the past few months. It looks like heroin is getting mixed with fentanyl and it's killing people. We've been investigating the Hokansons. We think they were planning to cash in with the music festival. With all of the people there, they'll have plenty of customers for their drugs. We tracked a stash of drugs to the ranch and they moved them this afternoon. You with me?" she asked.

Dane nodded. "Yes, ma'am." Shock showed on his face. "The Hokansons?"

Angela continued, "this afternoon, we think it was Clint, shot Agent Miller's dog and kidnapped an older guy from their cabin."

"Wow," Dane said.

"There's more," Angela said. "The older guy's named Cyrus. He's related to the Hokansons and he has a cell phone that we're tracking to see where he is." Angela paused, looked at Dane. "So, we're going to save Cyrus and if we can, grab some drugs and arrest the Hokansons."

"We believe he's alive," Dane said.

"Until we know different," Jack said. He walked over to the screen on the wall. He studied his phone with the image and held it up by the satellite map Angela was projecting. Then he jabbed his finger at the map. "He's right here."

Angela used the mapping software to drop a pin at the location Jack indicated and then enlarged the image. "Looks like an old farm," she said.

"Not the one my family investigated looking for Cyrus' gold," Jack said.

"Gold?" Dane asked.

"Another story. Another time," Angela said. "Looks like the barn's still standing. I'm betting that's where they are."

"What's the weather forecast?" Jack asked.

Angela pulled up the weather radar image. "Looks like the clouds and rain will be moving in for a while into the night."

"Dark and wet," Jack said. "Good hunting weather."

Dane tilted and turned his head towards Jack, a questioning look on his face.

"They'll be staying inside, all together," Jack said. "And if they aren't moving around, they might just fall asleep, making it easy for us to sneak up on them."

A silence followed. The radar image of the storm slowly advanced across the screen. Jack turned to the table. "We know they're armed. They shot Vince, my dog," he clarified for Dane. "They may have the barn stocked with weapons or brought some from their home with them. We're going to need radios so we can communicate, ballistic vests, flashlights, guns, and ammo." Jack tapped his holstered Glock, a reflex to make sure it was back where it belonged after being locked up for a few days.

Jack followed Dane to a closet and they grabbed the gear they'd need tonight. They carried it to the conference room and laid it out on the table. Angela stood at the monitor, studying the map. "I think it's pretty clear. There's one way in. We block that road so they can't leave in a vehicle and we surveil the barn."

"Who's in there besides Cyrus?" Jack asked.

"Clint, for sure, Otto, maybe Hanna." Angela stopped. "I think that's it. The family is hiding and leaving everyone else behind. And they wouldn't let anyone else into the secret they'd kidnapped Cyrus."

"Agreed," Jack said. "Your other officers?"

"Roger should be at the VFW. Adam's on duty. He's out in a car somewhere."

"Can Doris check where he's at? Make sure he's at the north or south end of town so he doesn't see us head out?"

"Sure. She can take care of that," Angela said.

Jack grabbed a ballistic vest and threw it on over his head. "Let's gear up and head out. Swing by the Hokanson's house on the way and then the State Park."

CHAPTER THIRTY-SIX

Thunder boomed and shook the barn. Rain pounded on the roof and steadily dripped in a couple of spots. They'd placed plastic buckets under the worst leaks. Others just dripped on the floor. It was going to be a wet night.

After a dinner of energy bars, salami and cheese sandwiches and apples, they blew up an air mattress for Hanna so she could rest. They put it in the corner of the barn, away from any falling water.

Otto poured some scotch into plastic cups and gave one to Cyrus. Then he sat down across from him. Clint grabbed a can of beer and sat with them. Otto considered telling Clint to leave, but decided to let him stay. If some force was needed, he'd leave it to Clint.

"I'm assuming this is the good stuff," Cyrus said.

"Of course." Otto held out his plastic cup, and Cyrus tapped his against it. "To family," Otto said.

Cyrus started laughing and then hacking, a deep cough from his chest. He got it under control and sipped the scotch. "To family, that was a good one."

"We are family," Otto said.

"Family," Cyrus spit on the floor. "Your dad and I were cousins by blood, barely. It wasn't family, just an accident of birth. You're my cousin once removed and those two," Cyrus flicked his hand at Hanna and Clint, "twice removed." He took another drink. "We're not family."

Otto needed to change tactics. He poured himself some more scotch and settled into his chair. "I heard good things about your mother."

Cyrus' eyes got big. He leaned forward and poked a finger towards Otto. "Don't talk about my mother."

"What? I said I heard good things about her. People said she was a great, young woman," Otto paused. "Until she met your father. She spread her legs like a cheap whore. Her brothers caught them in the act and chased him off."

Cyrus roared and struggled to get up out of his chair.

Clint jumped up and stood between him and Otto. "Sit down, old man." He stiff-armed Cyrus in the chest and he stumbled back into his chair.

"Just sit and listen, Cyrus. Clint, sit down." Otto took another drink. "They chased off your father and later discovered he'd grabbed a bag of gold the family had been saving. Some of it was your mother's. The rest is ours."

"There's no gold," Cyrus said. "You're grasping at straws. You can't run your legitimate businesses to make the profits you want. Your drug business is going nowhere. You haven't lived up to the Hokanson name."

Clint's phone rang. He answered it and walked to the barn doors to talk.

Cyrus continued, "Even if the gold was real and it's out there somewhere. I haven't been looking for it this summer. I have no need for it. I'm dying and I have no family. I'm the end of the line." This time it was Cyrus' turn for a drink. He sipped the scotch and leaned back in his chair. "Think about it. If there was gold and I knew about it, don't you think I would've come back long ago to get it so my wife and I could enjoy it?"

Otto studied Cyrus' face and his body language. He seemed relaxed and confident. What he said made sense. If there wasn't any gold and the drug business was a bust, for now, it was back to running their regular businesses. He and Hanna could run things going forward, enjoy time with the grandchild and plan something else for the future.

Otto took another drink. Clint was a problem. He shot the dog, kidnapped Cyrus. They wouldn't be holed up in this barn if it wasn't for him.

Cyrus broke into his thoughts. "Looks like you're trying to figure things out. You're in quite the predicament. Why don't you just let me go."

Otto got up out of his chair. "I can't do that. At least not yet. I have to figure some things out. Sit tight. I'll be right back." He walked over to check on Hanna. He found her relaxing on the air mattress. "Are you doing OK?" he asked.

Hanna rolled over on and put her hands on her stomach. "I don't know if it's what we ate tonight or what, but I have some indigestion."

"Can I get you anything?" Otto asked.

"No. But how long are we going to stay here?"

Otto yawned and exhaled heavily. "We'll take it a day at a time. Not too long."

Hanna sighed. "OK."

Clint yelled from the other end of the barn. "Dad!"

"I'm back with Hanna," Otto replied.

Clint joined them. "Good news. The Red Lake gang will buy the drugs. They wanted to screw me on price, but I said I could deliver tomorrow for the original price."

"Nice job, brother," Hanna mumbled.

Clint pointed at Hanna. "Is she OK?" he asked.

"She doesn't feel good," Otto said. He nodded towards the middle of the barn. "Let's go talk."

Otto and Clint walked past Cyrus to the vehicle. "Nice job finding a buyer for the drugs," Otto said. He put his hand on Clint's shoulder. "I think you have to go, right now."

"Now?" Clint asked.

A vision formed in Otto's mind. He still had a chance to save the Hokanson family, Hanna and her baby. If he let Clint go. "Yes, you need to go now. Nobody knows this truck, it's dark, it's raining. You head out now for the Red Lake Reservation and you'll be there in three or four hours."

"But, what about you guys?"

"We'll be OK. Now listen to me. You're leaving and you're not coming back for a while," Otto said.

"What?" Clint stepped back from Otto. "What are you talking about?"

"Clint, listen," Otto said in a calm voice. "You kidnapped a man. You shot an FBI agent's dog and people have been dying. You need to get away from here."

"And go where?"

"Stay on the reservation for a little while. See if they can help get you into Canada."

Clint paced back and forth. "I don't know." He pulled out a cigarette and lit it. "What about him?" He pointed at Cyrus.

"Leave him here with us. He's still OK. No harm's been done to him." Otto thought about how they'd spin a tale, even though Cyrus would contradict him. But they saved him from Clint. That's how it would come out.

"I'm afraid if you don't do this you won't be free," Otto said. "Take it a step at a time. Get to Red Lake. They have to have connections in Canada. It's only a couple of hours north with a lightly guarded border." Otto stepped forward and wrapped Clint in a hug. "I want you to be safe."

"OK," Clint said in his ear. "You're right. I'll do it."

CHAPTER THIRTY-SEVEN

The Hokanson home was empty. The beacon on Jack's phone still showed Julie's phone in the same spot on the map. Jack hoped it was with Cyrus. He was doubting his decision to wait on their rescue of Cyrus and to not bring in more officers, but who could they trust?

Angela drove into Maplewood State Park. The windshield wipers swept back and forth, clearing the raindrops from the glass. The headlights illuminated a ranger's pickup parked across the road at the entrance.

"What's this?" Jack asked.

"I had to call the rangers and tell them what was going on. We can't have campers get in our way or panic if there's shooting," Angela said. "I'll be right back." She walked up to the pickup and spoke with the ranger inside.

"What are you thinking, Dane?" Jack asked.

"I'm nervous. I'm ready. We have to save this guy if he's alive."

"He's alive," Jack said. "Until we know he isn't."

"Right," Dane said.

Angela rejoined them in their truck. "They have rangers at the exit of each campground road to keep people from leaving. And the one posted here." She pulled a folded piece of paper out from inside her jacket and handed it to Jack. "The ranger marked a gravel service road that gets us close." The pickup in front of them backed up to let them through. "Let's go," she said.

They wound through the park road in the rain. Angela turned off the headlights when they reached the gravel road, turned in, parked, and shut off the truck.

"We hoof it from here," Jack said. "The rain and thunder should cover any sounds we make as we approach. How far?"

"Ranger said about a quarter of a mile to where there's another grass drive through some trees back to the barn," Angela said.

"OK. First, we try to see if we can get close enough to see who's there. Verify if Cyrus is there. Then, we'll figure out what we're going to do next. Ready?" Jack asked.

They each checked their gear and weapons. Angela handed her keys to Dane. "In case we need the truck."

"Got it," Dane said.

"Let's go," Jack said.

They climbed out their doors of the truck and carefully shut them to minimize the noise. "I'm going first," Angela said. She led the way as the three walked single file along the wet gravel road.

Jack's senses came alive as his vision was cut to almost nothing in the wet darkness. The crunch of their boots on the gravel and the rain splattering on their hats and coats sounded like a loud concert to him. He knew they were quiet among the rest of the noises of the night.

He caught sight of things in his peripheral vision and turned his head from side to side, scanning the road ahead to see. Angela continued forward. He heard Dane behind him. Angela stopped. Jack and Dane joined her.

"This is the grassy drive into the barn," Angela said.

There was a wall of tall weeds with a path knocked down through the middle of them. If it hadn't been raining, they might have sprung back up and hidden the drive.

Jack was impressed with how Angela took control. She wanted this. It had probably been a long time coming, taking down the Hokansons.

"Dane, you stay here. Nobody comes out or in. We'll let you know if we need help or the truck. You're our last line of defense."

"Got it," Dane said.

They checked their radios to make sure they were working, and then Angela turned and headed into the weeds. Jack clapped Dane on the back and said, "See you soon. Stay alert," and followed Angela.

As Angela and Jack approached the barn, they slowed. They crept forward a couple of steps and then stopped to observe. Jack inched up close to Angela and whispered in her ear, "We have to get closer and see if we can see or hear anything."

A few spots of light leaked out from cracks in the walls of the barn. Jack and Angela split up to approach from different directions. Angela headed for the closed doors of the barn and Jack for the side where the light was coming through the walls. The same rain noises that hid their approach covered up any sounds from the barn. Jack had to get closer to see if he could hear anything.

He crept through the weeds and bushes and worked his way up next to the barn. Light leaked out some of the cracks in the walls, but he couldn't see in. He put his ear up against the wooden side of the barn. The wood was rough and wet.

He smelled cigarettes. He heard voices. An argument or a heated discussion? He couldn't make out the words, but the tone of the voices sounded like Otto and Clint. Where was Cyrus?

He keyed his radio. "Angela. I hear a couple of voices. Maybe Clint and Otto. Can't tell what they're saying. I smelled cigarettes. Guessing Clint's inside. How about you?"

Jack heard in his ear, "it's quiet out here. Nothing at this end of the barn. Doors are closed. Wondering if we should go in or let them know we're here."

"Hang on," Jack answered. "I'm moving positions." Jack moved along the wall away from Angela, towards the rear of the barn. He stopped and tried to see or hear what was going on inside again. Still nothing. The voices were harder to hear. "Moving again," Jack said into his mic.

Jack considered his options: call Julie's cell phone and maybe they'd answer and he could negotiate with Otto, or he and Angela storm in through the door, or wait them out, or make noise at this end of the barn to distract them inside so Angela could go in the main doors. "Have any ideas?" he asked Angela over the radio.

"I'm still watching the doors. Wondering how long we wait. Offense or defense? We waiting or going in? Cyrus might need us."

"Let me check out one more spot." Jack moved along the wall. It looked like there might be a window. Inching along the wall, his foot hit something hard, he tripped and fell into the side of the barn. His shoulder hit the wall and he fell into the wet weeds. He heard loud voices from in the barn. "Angela, get ready. I tripped. They heard me."

Jack pushed himself up and ran for the barn doors, hoping not to trip again.

"I'm going in," he heard in his ear.

"Angela, wait," he replied." He pushed through the brush and broke through by the corner of the barn. The doors were open. Time for offense.

He peeked around the door into the barn, holding his Glock in his left hand. Not his dominant hand, but he'd practiced shooting left-handed. He readied to shoot. An old Suburban was pointed nose out. Angela used it for cover. A new voice spoke into his ear, "this is Dane. Do you need me?"

Jack responded, "get in the truck, start it up, drive it up to the grass drive. We'll let you know. Be ready."

Angela crouched at the front bumper of the truck. "It's the Police! Put your hands in the air and move to the center of the barn!" she yelled.

Clint stood at the back of the truck. Its doors were open. Otto stood beyond him, farther back in the barn. Cyrus sat in a chair, smiling. He's OK, Jack thought. Relieved that the old guy was still with them.

Jack pushed the door shut a few feet to get a better angle on the inside while he peeked around it, using it for a shield. The guns the Hokansons had wouldn't put a bullet through this old hard oak. "Otto! You heard what she said!" he yelled into the barn. He wanted to let Otto and Clint know Angela wasn't alone.

Clint disappeared into the back of the truck. A few seconds later he reappeared and something flew through the air towards Angela. It trailed a cloud of white and exploded in a puff of powder, filling the air when it hit the hood of the truck. It bounced and landed at Angela's feet. It looked like a brick of drugs to Jack.

Angela fell backward, scrambling to get away from the cloud.

A roar sounded from the barn and Cyrus jumped up, dragging the chair attached to his ankle by a length of rope as he charged Clint.

Otto raised his arm and aimed his gun at Cyrus' back.

"No!" Jack yelled. Two explosions filled the air as Otto and Jack fired.

Cyrus wrapped Clint in a bear hug and drove him into the back of the truck. Otto fell to the ground. A scream filled the air from farther back in the barn. "Daddy!"

Jack spied Angela on the floor of the barn, dragging herself back towards the doors. She appeared to be weakening and then slumped back onto the floor. Jack sucked in a lungful of air in case there were still drugs floating around in the barn and rushed in. He made it to Angela's side. She was breathing, but she didn't respond to his questions. Jack glanced into the barn to make sure there wasn't a threat and grabbed Angela by her vest and dragged her out into the rain. He hoped the rain would wash the heroin or fentanyl powder away.

"Dane, get your truck up here now," Jack said into his radio. "We need some transport to the hospital. Hurry. Angela's down. She inhaled some drugs, heroin or something."

"On my way."

Jack crouched over Angela. Her breathing was shallow. She grunted, struggling to breathe. Her eyes were closed. "Angela, wake up." He patted her on the cheek. She didn't respond. He searched her vest pockets and found a plastic package of Narcan in one of them. He ripped it open and remembered what Angela had done at the street dance. He tilted her head back, stuck the nozzle of the device in one of her nostrils and pushed the plunger with his thumb, hoping it worked.

Jack patted her cheeks a little harder and shook her. "Come on Angela, you with me?" He rolled her onto her side and slapped her on the back. "Angela, wake up."

She sucked in a breath and opened her eyes. "Angela, you OK?" Jack asked. "Welcome back."

She nodded slowly and looked at Jack, a confused look on her face.

Jack pulled her up into a seated position. "Wait here. Don't move," he said. He keyed his mic. "Dane, Angela's sitting in front of the barn. Just gave her some Narcan. She's awake. Take care of her. I'm going into the barn."

Jack grabbed his Glock and headed into the barn to check on Cyrus and the others. Hanna stood over Otto, screaming.

Otto was breathing. Jack's shot had hit him in the right shoulder. Jack picked up Otto's gun and stood over him. "It's over," Jack said. Otto nodded.

"Hanna, sit on the ground next to your dad." Jack helped her sit on the floor. Her crotch was soaked. He grabbed Otto's wrists and handcuffed them together over his belly. Then he ripped off a piece of Otto's shirt and placed it on the wound. "Hanna, listen to me." She sucked in some breaths as she cried. Jack took her hand and placed it on the cloth over the wound. "Hold this here. I'll be right back."

Jack turned his attention to Cyrus and Clint. Clint was on the ground. His face covered in white powder. His tongue hung out the corner of his mouth and his eyes were open, unresponsive.

Cyrus lay next to him, gasping. His back was covered in blood. Jack knelt next to him. "Hey, you OK?"

Cyrus coughed and gasped. "No. I think," he coughed. "I think I've been shot."

Jack rolled Cyrus onto his back and held his hand. "Otto shot you. Clint's dead. That's quite the family you have."

Angela stumbled over and joined them. Cyrus weakly smiled at her. "Is he OK?" she asked Jack. Jack shook his head.

"Damn it," Cyrus rasped out. He licked his lips and

coughed. "They're not my family." He looked at Angela and then at Jack. He squeezed Jack's hand. "You are." Cyrus gasped and some blood trickled from the corner of his mouth. A breath rattled from his lungs and his head slumped to the side. His grasp grew weak in Jack's hand.

Jack held onto Cyrus' hand. "Goodbye, buddy," he said. He checked Cyrus' pulse and felt nothing. Then he placed Cyrus' hands over his chest and stood.

Angela stood next to him, tears streaming down her face. Jack put an arm around her shoulder and wiped tears from his own eyes. Dane attended to Otto and Hanna.

Jack sucked in a breath and blew it out. "OK, you go get in the truck," he said to Angela. "I'll help Dane."

Angela stumbled back to the truck outside. Jack helped Dane get Otto to his feet. "I'll take Otto," Jack said to Dane. "You help Hanna."

Jack held Otto by his left elbow and guided him to the truck. "Clint's dead," he said to Otto.

"I figured," Otto said.

"Looks like your grandchild will be visiting you in prison. Not quite how you thought things were going to turn out, I bet."

Otto shook his head.

Jack and Dane got Angela settled in the front seat and Otto and Hanna in the back. Outside the truck, Jack gave Dane some instructions. "You're in charge. Call the hospital and tell them to get ready. You've got an overdose victim revived with Narcan, a gunshot victim and a pregnant woman whose water just broke. I'll grab the crime scene tape and secure the area and call the Bureau of Criminal Apprehension and get them out here to investigate. After you get them settled, come back out here with some coffee and we'll wait for the BCA to release the crime scene to them."

"Got it," Dane said. "See you soon."

Jack watched as Dane turned the truck around and headed away from the barn. He didn't move. He thought about how he was going to break the news about Cyrus to his family. Once he was ready. He watched the taillights disappear through the brush and stood in the rain, letting it wash the events of the night and the tears away.

CHAPTER THIRTY-EIGHT

"Hi, guys," Angela called out as she approached Julie and Jack standing at the smoking grill.

Vince whined from his resting spot next to the grill. Angela stopped and bent over to pet him. "No need to get up. You rest."

"Good timing. The burgers are about ready," Jack said. "How are you feeling?"

"I'm fine. I was a little wiped out, but I'm feeling OK now. The doctor said to relax for a couple of days and then I should be fine."

"You need anything to drink?" Jack asked.

"I'm good with water for now." Angela held up her bottle of water. "How's everybody doing here? With Cyrus' passing, I mean"

Julie answered. "A little sad. I think tonight's farewell will help." She put an arm around Angela's shoulder and gave her a little hug.

"The kids haven't lost someone before," Jack said. "It's hard to tell with kids. But, I'm going to miss the old fart."

"I don't know if I ever figured him out," Angela said.

"Doris gave me an envelope today that Cyrus asked her to pass on to me if he died."

"Really?" Julie said. "What was in it?"

"It contained a note directing me to talk with an attorney here in town. I met with her today and Cyrus left instructions on disposal of his ashes and another little mystery for us."

"He's full of mystery," Jack said.

"Let's get the kids up here for supper and we'll talk about it while we eat," Julie said.

"Nice job with the burgers, Jack," Julie said.

"And the corn on the cob is done to perfection," Angela added.

"Yes, nice job, Dad," Lynn said.

Willy had an ear of corn up to his mouth. He smiled and gave Jack a thumbs up.

"Thanks. I think I'm getting the hang of it." Jack sat at the head of the table. He listened to the noises on the lake. Vince had found his way under the table, waiting for something to drop. It felt good to have him home to recover with them.

Eating dinner with his family hadn't been a regular thing. Jack often didn't get home in time when he was working and he definitely wasn't home early enough to make dinner on the grill. He needed to make more time for things like this. Maybe working in the corporate world he would have more regular hours. Something to think about.

Jack picked up his beer. "I think we should toast who we're here to honor tonight." He raised his bottle and looked at the other end of the table. The kids had set a place for Cyrus. They'd placed the wooden box of ashes Angela had brought with her on the seat. A Swisher Sweet cigar rested next to the napkin and cutlery. They were ready to say goodbye.

"To Cyrus. A man I will never forget, a hero from wars past and recent, a storyteller," Jack paused. He felt the emotion pressing in his chest. He blinked his eyes and drew in a deep breath, held it and blew it out. Then he continued, "A man who taught me how to fish and some other valuable life lessons." His voice hitched. Jack paused again before saying, "A man who I call my friend."

"To Cyrus," Julie answered. They all reached around the table, clinking their bottles and glasses against each other's.

"To Cyrus," they all repeated.

Julie dabbed at her eyes with her napkin. "Whew, it's hard to say goodbye," she said. "I think we should all share a memory. I'll go first." Julie turned and addressed the empty chair. "Cyrus, I want to thank you for showing us the beauty of this area where you were born and for sharing your stories around the fire."

Willy said, "I'll go next." He wiped the butter and corn kernels from his lips. "Cyrus, I want to thank you for helping to solve our mystery and teaching me how to fish."

Lynn followed. "I want to thank you for your stories and the metal detector and for solving our mystery."

The kids looked at Angela. She wiped her eyes and shook her head. "I'll go last."

"OK, I'll go." Jack pushed back his chair, stood and faced across the table. "Cyrus, you are my friend and I thank you for showing me the importance of family, though your own family was kind of a mess. I'm sorry we didn't get to meet your wife. I will think of you often."

Jack reached into his pocket and felt the ring. "And I also thank you for the metal detector. Because without it I wouldn't have found this." Jack pulled the ring from his pocket, grabbed Julie's left hand in his and got down on one knee. He stared into Julie's eyes. The words he'd been practicing for this moment didn't seem adequate. He cleared his throat and then spoke, "Julie Miller, the love of my life, the mother of our two beautiful children, you put up with so much from me and make me such a better person. You are more than I deserve and I count my blessings every day that we're together. Will you continue to be my wife?"

Julie nodded and said, "Yes."

Jack slipped the ring on to her finger, stood and pulled her up from her chair. He wrapped his arms around her and kissed her fully on the lips.

Lynn clapped and cheered. Willy turned his head away and smiled. Angela whistled and cheered.

Julie leaned back from his grasp. "How long have you had that ring? And you didn't give it back to me?"

Jack smirked. "I wanted to find the right time. With everything going on, that time never came. Tonight seemed like the right time."

"It was," Julie said. She kissed him. "Thank you." She pried herself from his hug and sat down in her seat. Holding her hand up, she rubbed the ring with her other hand. "It feels good to have it back."

Jack sat in his seat. "Whew," he said, and smiled. "I'm glad she said yes."

"Angela hasn't shared her Cyrus memory with us," Lynn said.

Julie said, "I'm sorry you were so rudely interrupted, Angela. What's your memory."

Angela smiled. "My memory is the first time I met Cyrus and you, Jack." She tilted her water bottle towards the box of ashes and then at him. "At the park, fighting Clint."

Laughing, Jack said, "My introduction to the Hokansons. That's what started the adventure of this whole past week."

"If you call this past week an adventure," Julie said.

Angela tipped her bottle and finished it. Then she stood up. "Well, I might have an adventure for us." She picked up the envelope that she'd brought with her. "Cyrus left some additional information for us about spreading his ashes."

"At the state park, right?" Jack said.

"Close," Angela said. "And he's given us another mystery to solve."

Lynn jumped up. "What is it?"

"One thing at a time," Angela said.

"Are we taking the boat?" Julie asked.

Angela nodded. "Of course."

Julie rallied the troops. "Jack, you take Cyrus' ashes down to the boat and get it ready to go. Kids, clear the table."

Jack slipped part of a burger under the table to Vince. "Watch the place while we're gone, buddy."

"And then can you help me carry these duffels to the boat?" Angela asked Lynn and Willy. "They're an important part of the mystery."

"Let's go!" Willy said. "I love mysteries." He jumped up and started to clear the table.

THE SUN HAD STARTED to set. It was still above the trees. Jack drove the boat out onto the calm lake. "Where are we going?" he asked.

"Not far," Angela said. "The little cabin on the west side of the island."

"Isn't that private property?" Jack asked.

"It is, but we have permission to go there tonight."

"OK, let's go," Jack said. It was less than a mile in the boat. Willy and Lynn worked on Angela, trying to get her to give up the mystery. Julie sat next to Jack and held the box containing Cyrus' ashes. Jack reached over and squeezed her hand.

Jack guided the boat up to the shore. An old cabin sat back in the trees. Jack grabbed a rope that was attached to a cleat on the front of the boat and stepped from the open bow onto the grass. Then he helped everyone else from the boat, one by one.

The group gathered together on the grass facing west. "This is a beautiful view," Julie said.

"This is where Cyrus wanted his ashes scattered?" Jack asked.

"This is part of the mystery," Angela said. She turned to the cabin behind them. "One thing I learned, this cabin, this island, belonged to Cyrus' mother."

"What?" Julie said. "Keeping secrets," she said to the box she held.

"Cyrus shared that with me," Jack said. "Family secret."

"Way back, when the family had some money and split it among the children, she used her money to buy this property and to build this cabin," Angela said. "Cyrus would like his ashes to be spread from the cabin to the lake and into the water."

Julie led the group back towards the cabin. "It's time to say goodbye." She opened the wooden box and the plastic bag inside that held the ashes.

Jack put his hands in the bag and grabbed a couple of handfuls of ash. "Full of mystery until the end, my friend," he said and sprinkled the ash in the grass in front of the cabin. "Welcome home."

Julie moved towards the lake and Angela, Lynn and Willy took turns spreading ashes in the grass. At the lake, Julie spread the remaining ashes from the bag into the water. "Thank you, Cyrus," she said. "We'll miss you."

The group gathered in front of the cabin again. "This is a beautiful view," Julie said. The sun streamed through the clouds in the west, turning the sky shades of red and orange.

"I think Cyrus is going to like it," Lynn said.

Angela stepped forward and turned to face the group. "And I am too."

"What?" Julie said.

"It's another part of the Cyrus mystery. This place was his mother's, and then his. He left it to me."

CHAPTER THIRTY-NINE

Jack chuckled. "I don't mean to be a killjoy, but you have seen this place, right?" The cabin had been a victim to the elements of Minnesota summers and winters for some time. The screen door hung from one hinge, screens on the windows were torn and the roof was missing shingles in spots.

"It needs a little TLC," Angela said.

"A lot," Jack said under his breath.

"OK, more than a little," Angela said. "But you've seen the lake and the view. It's a beautiful spot."

"That's going to take some time and money," Jack said.

Angela nodded and looked at Jack. She pulled a few sheets of paper from the envelope the lawyer had given her. Then she smiled and winked at the kids. "We all know Cyrus had some stories, and they seemed to be based on some truths, like the dog license story."

"Or the gold story," Willy said.

"Well, Cyrus has left me another story, or mystery, to share with you all tonight," Angela said.

"What is it?" Lynn asked.

"All will be revealed," Angela said. "Can you guys go grab the duffel bags from the boat?"

Willy took off running for the boat. "I'll get one," he said. Lynn ran along behind them.

Jack threw a questioning look at Angela. "What's going on?"

Angela smirked. "Cyrus isn't done with us yet."

Willy and Lynn came running back from the boat, dragging the duffels through the grass. "These are heavy," Willy said. "What's in them?"

"Thanks, guys," Angela said. "That's just some stuff we might need." She knelt in the grass by Willy and Lynn and pulled out a folded piece of paper. "Here we have a treasure map." She unfolded it and smoothed it out on the grass.

"Cool!" Willy said.

"Who made it?" Lynn asked.

"I'm pretty sure Cyrus made it this summer," Angela answered.

"Wait," Willy said. "It looks like the island." He pointed at the paper. "Here's the cabin."

"Where's the treasure?" Lynn asked.

"I think like the pirates say, X marks the spot," Angela said. She handed the paper to Lynn. "Why don't you guys see if you can find it."

Willy and Lynn looked over the map and then jumped up and ran towards the cabin.

Angela picked up one of the duffels. "I think we're going to need these. Grab the other one," she said to Jack.

Jack hefted the bag up and put the strap over his shoulder. "What do you have in these?"

"You'll see," Angela answered, and she walked after the kids.

Jack grabbed Julie's hand and smiled at her. He felt the

ring on the finger. It felt good to have it back in place. "Guess we should go join them."

Julie pulled her hand from his and laughed. "I'm not going to miss this. Hurry up," she said and ran after the kids.

When Jack caught up with the group behind the cabin, they were gathered around a rusted square steel door covering a hole in the ground. A shiny silver padlock secured it, locking the lid to a rusted metal ring.

"It was kind of hidden, Dad, but we found it," Willy said. "It was covered by bushes and dead sticks."

"Nice job, guys," Jack said. "But, it's locked."

Angela smiled. "Somebody gave me a key." She handed the key to Lynn. "Why don't you unlock it."

Lynn took the key and fit it into the lock and unlocked it. She removed the padlock and looked up at her parents.

"Let's see what's inside," Julie said. "Be careful."

Willy and Lynn lifted the edge of the rusty door and swung it up. Its hinges squealed in response. They flipped the door all the way open and dropped the door onto the grass.

"Careful," Julie repeated.

They'd revealed a black opening in the ground. A musty smell came up from its depths.

"Have a flashlight?" Jack asked.

Angela pulled one from the bag and handed it to Jack. He shone it down into the hole. The black hole sucked up the light, revealing very little. Jack dropped a rock into the hole and heard a splash.

"What is this?" Lynn asked.

"An old cistern, I think," Jack said.

"What's a cistern," Willy asked.

"It's like a water tank," Jack said. "For when people lived here. They'd capture rainwater and store it here to use, along with the lake water."

Angela knelt next to her duffels and unzipped them. "It's

also the site of our treasure hunt," she said. She pulled some ropes and harnesses from the duffels along with a hard hat with a headlamp, gloves and safety glasses. The last thing she pulled out was Cyrus' metal detector.

"Are you going in, Jack?" Angela asked.

Julie laughed, "Him? No way. He's claustrophobic."

Jack shook his head slightly. "Yeah, I'm not going in there."

Angela grabbed the harness. "Then I guess it's me." She pulled the harness up her legs and secured it around her waist. Then she grabbed the rope. She attached one end to the harness. She found a sturdy tree close to the opening and attached a nylon strap to it and ran the rope through that. "Think you guys together can hold me?" she asked.

"Sure," Willy answered. "We'll help, Dad."

Angela put on the hard hat and glasses, turned on the headlamp, grabbed the metal detector, turned it on and walked to the lip of the hole. "Time to find some treasure. You guys grab the rope and lower me down. I'm not sure how deep this cistern is or how deep the water in it is. I'm hoping I can stand in it and walk around." She sat down on the lip of the hole. Jack and his family pulled the rope tight. "Here I go," Angela said ,and she slipped over the lip into the cistern.

The rope stretched as Angela went over the lip. Jack held tight and listened for instructions.

"You can slowly let me down," Angela said, her muffled voice coming up from the ground.

Jack, Julie, and the kids let out some rope, lowering Angela further into the hole. The line went slack. "She must've found the bottom," Jack said.

"OK, give me some more slack. I'm going to walk around down here," Angela said.

The foursome let go of the rope and stepped to the lip of the hole to see what Angela was up to. Jack saw the headlamp reflect off the water and illuminate the walls of the cistern. They were covered with moss, and roots protruded out of cracks. Angela swung the metal detector back and forth in front of her. Along the north wall, they heard a beep. Then it got stronger. "I've got something," Angela called up.

"OK," Jack yelled down into the hole. "We'll pull you up."

"Wait," Angela replied. "There are supposed to be two bags." She held a green cloth bag by its handles out of the water. "I have to keep looking." The light from her headlamp followed along the wall. She swept the detector back and forth through the water. At the southeast corner, she stopped and pulled up another green bag. She walked back and stood under the opening, a big smile on her face. "OK, you can pull me up now."

"This is going to be harder," Jack said. "Lifting is harder, plus we don't know what treasure she's picked up." He looped the rope in his hand. The kids and Julie grabbed the line and they all pulled, lifting Angela from the bottom of the cistern. Grunting and heaving, they lifted her high enough to see a gloved hand come up through the hole and grab onto the lip.

"The kids and I will hold her, Julie," Jack said. "Go see if you can help get her out of there."

"I'm coming, Angela," Julie yelled.

"Hold on kids," Jack said. They kept the line taut as Julie helped pull Angela up and out of the hole.

Jack traded high-fives with the kids and they went over to join Julie and Angela in the grass next to the cistern. Angela's pants were wet up past the knees. Her boots were covered in muck. "Something stinks," Willy said.

"Yeah, sorry," Angela said. "It was pretty bad down there. Lots of mud and stagnant water." She peeled the harness off and stomped her feet in the grass. The green bags she'd found were sitting next to her feet.

"What's in the bags?" Lynn asked.

Dusk was winning, and it was getting darker back behind the cabin next to the cistern. "Cyrus' note said that the best stories were told around the fire at your cabin. Let's put all of the gear away, lock up the cistern, head back to your cabin and I'll finish Cyrus' story and let you know what's in the bags."

CHAPTER FORTY

J ack, Willy, and Lynn worked on getting the fire started. Angela changed into some clean clothes. Julie got together some beverages and chips to snack on and joined Jack and the kids at the fire.

"Chief Angela, the fire is started," Lynn yelled towards the cabin.

"I'm here," Angela said. She walked towards the fire carrying a green bag by its handle in each hand.

"Sit here," Willy said, pointing to the Adirondack chair in the middle of the group of chairs. "That's where Cyrus sat when he told his stories."

"Seems fitting," Angela said. She sat in the chair and set the bags at her feet.

The fire danced in the pit. Jack wondered what Angela was going to share. He had an idea it had something to do with the gold based on what she'd said earlier. But what? The bags Angela carried appeared heavy.

Julie passed out some snacks and drinks to everyone. "OK, I think we're ready," she said.

"I'll start," Angela said. "I'm probably not the storyteller

Cyrus was, but I can tell you about the info and letter he left me." She closed her eyes for a couple of seconds and then opened them and began. "Cyrus told you a family story about Civil War gold. It was a story he heard growing up and one his mom repeated to him. We've all wondered what Cyrus was doing back here this summer after being gone his whole life. He came back to find the gold. Not that he wanted or needed it at his age, but he didn't want the Hokansons to ever have it."

"Smart man," Jack said. "Did he find it?"

"He did," Angela said. "He kept it a secret, until now." She reached down and unzipped the green bags. Then she tipped them and emptied them onto the grass. The sound of pinging metal filled the night. The firelight reflected off of rectangular bricks in the grass.

There was silence. The only sound was the crackling of the fire. Then Julie spoke, "What is that, Angela?"

"Is that what I think it is?" Jack asked.

"It depends what you think it is," Angela answered, her smile showing in her voice.

Jack got out of his chair, stepped over to Angela's and picked up one of the bricks. It was smooth to the touch. The light of the fire made it look yellow or gold. Jack tilted the brick toward the fire, looking for markings. "This isn't the gold," he said.

"I think it is," Angela said. "Cyrus said it was. There are twenty, two-pound ingots here."

Jack whistled.

"Come here, kids," Angela said. Help me stack these up in piles, four ingots in each."

Willy and Lynn jumped out of their chairs and sat in the grass by Angela's feet. "Give me that one, Dad," Lynn said. She and Willy stacked the ingot into five piles, four in each.

"OK, Cyrus gave me some instructions on what to do

with the gold he found," Angela said. "He gifted eight to Pelican Rapids," Angela said. "I'll be getting those to the mayor and the city council to use for the good of the town. Besides gifting me the island and the cabin, he gifted me four ingots to use for rebuilding the cabin."

"Eight and four, that's twelve," Lynn said. "There are eight more."

"Yep," Angelas said. She picked up four ingots in each hand and smiled. She looked at the kids sitting in the grass. "Cyrus really enjoyed spending his last days with all of you. He didn't have any kids or grandkids of his own." She held out her hands. "Take these, they're getting heavy." Willy and Lynn each took four ingots in their cupped hands. "Cyrus gave you each one of the stacks to help pay for college."

"What?" Julie gasped. "We can't accept that," she said, and turned to Jack. "Can we?" She turned back to Angela. "How much is it?"

Angela laughed. "Each ingot is worth about fifty thousand."

"Wow," Julie said.

Smiling, her white teeth bright in the firelight, Angela said, "He got the last laugh on the Hokansons."

Jack shook his head and smiled.

"What?" Julie said. "Wow."

ANGELA, Jack, Julie and the kids sat watching the fire. The night took over. The light of the moon and the stars filled the sky. The kids played with the ingots, the metal ringing as they shuffled them into piles. Jack couldn't believe what Cyrus had done. He reached over and squeezed Julie's hand. She turned to him and he whispered, "Wow," and smiled.

Jack's cell phone vibrated in his pocket. He reflexively grabbed for it. Julie frowned. Checking the caller ID he showed the screen to her. It was Linda; the headhunter, calling.

Julie took the phone from Jack. "I told her to call tonight. She'd be able to get a hold of you," she said. She hit the speaker button, "Hello, Linda."

"Hi, Julie. Is Jack available?"

"We're sitting around the fire and I have the phone on speaker. He can hear you." Julie held the phone on an open palm between them.

"Jack?"

"Hi, Linda. I'm here," Jack said.

"Sorry to bother you, but Julie said tonight would be a good chance to catch you. I have two strong contenders vying for your services. Both are headquartered in Minneapolis. They're similar money and benefits, I think you'd be happy. But we need to get a time set up for you to meet them so you can have the info and exposure to decide which one might be a better environment, which one you feel is a better fit."

"Well Linda," Jack started. Julie put her finger up to her lips, signaling him to be quiet.

"Linda, this is Julie. Thanks for all of your work in narrowing down these opportunities. We've had an interesting start to our vacation," she paused, "and we've learned that Jack isn't ready to leave the FBI."

Jack shot Julie a look of surprise and smiled.

"Thanks again, Linda," Julie said, and ended the call. She tossed Jack's phone back in the grass, away from the group.

"Wow, again," Jack said. He got up out of his chair, pulled Julie to her feet wrapped his arms around her and kissed her, a long passionate kiss.

"Wow," Julie said, and laughed.

"It's been quite a night," Jack said, looking into her eyes.

"Yes, it has been quite a night," Angela said. "Can you kids help me put twelve of the ingots into one of these bags?"

Willy and Lynn counted out and placed twelve ingots in one of the green bags. Julie gave Angela a hug. "Thank you," she said.

"Thank Cyrus," Angela said.

Jack gave Angela a hug. "We'll see you at the festival tomorrow."

"Yes," she said. "I'll be there."

"Drive home safe tonight. You have a valuable cargo."

CHAPTER FORTY-ONE

Jack followed a line of cars into the gravel drive. The kids sat in the back seat, excited to attend the festival. The ranch was hopping with people; the sun was shining and country music filled the air. "Everybody has sunscreen on?" Julie asked.

"Yes, Mom," Willy and Lynn each answered.

"I'm mostly worried about your dad."

"Yes, Mom," Jack said. "I have sunscreen on and I brought a hat."

After parking, the family walked into the tent filled arena. The kids ran to the tent with face painting. Jack and Julie held hands and followed along. Lynn got a pelican on her cheek and Willy got a walleye on his. "I see the summer vacation theme," Jack said.

"Can we get something to eat?" Lynn asked.

"Sure, but not too much," Jack said. "I don't want you to be so full that you can't dance with me when the live music starts."

They huddled, trying to decide what they wanted for lunch.

"Hey, guys," Angela interrupted them. "I'm so glad you're here."

"Hi," Julie said, and she gave her a hug.

"We were wondering if we'd run into you with all of these people here," Jack said. "There's a great turnout."

"I know. It looks like it's going to be a success," Angela said.

"Are you performing?" Willy asked.

"Yes," Angela said. "Later in the show." Angela put her hands in her pockets and shifted her weight from foot to foot. Jack recognized the sign. She wasn't saying something that she needed to say.

"Is there something else, Chief?" Jack asked.

"Umm, there's something else I didn't tell you last night."

"What else could there be?" Julie asked.

"Well, after the success with stopping the Hokansons and their drug ring, and with the Fargo FBI agents investigating the Otter Tail County sheriff's office, some of the county commissioners have asked me to run for Sheriff in the upcoming election. And I've decided to run. I love Pelican Rapids, but I'd love to serve the people of the entire county." Angela pulled some stickers from her pocket. "Anybody want to wear one of these for me today?" The stickers said *Rancone For Sheriff - Otter Tail County* on them.

"I do," Willy said.

"I'll take one," Lynn said.

Angela handed them each a sticker and they placed them on their chests.

"We'd be proud to wear them," Julie said. "Anything else we can do to help?"

Angela pointed down the row of tents. "My campaign table is down at the end. Maybe grab a few fliers and pass them out?"

Jack slapped a sticker on his own chest. "You'll make a great sheriff." He opened his arms wide to give her a hug. He wrapped her in his arms. "Congratulations," he whispered in her ear. "Please don't call me for any help this next week. We're on vacation."

AFTERWORD

People wonder where I get the ideas for my stories. There's a scene in this story where Jack's wife loses her wedding ring in the lake.

This happened to my wife and I in real life. And we found a 1942 dog license tag while we searched for the ring with a metal detector.

That started the question, how did that old dog license get in the lake? The first scene I wrote when I was creating the story was the one Cyrus tells around the campfire about the man getting chased by the dog.

And the rest of the story is Twice Removed.

ACKNOWLEDGMENTS

I have to thank my writing group. We meet every two weeks on Monday night, critiquing each other's work. In particular, I have to thank Dawn, a member we lost to cancer. She always gave me the feedback to not be so nice.

In addition, I have to thank Ross and Liliana Bowen. At a Alzheimer's Association Gala they purchased the naming of a character. Sheriff Angela Rancone was born from this gift to the Alzheimer's Association and the work they do.

ABOUT THE AUTHOR

Douglas Dorow lives in Minneapolis, Minnesota with his wife and their two dogs.

Twice Removed is the second book in his FBI thriller series following The Ninth District.

Contact me via email at Doug@DouglasDorow.com

I'd appreciate a review at your favorite online ebook retailer.

Read, for the THRILL of it!

ALSO BY DOUGLAS DOROW

For updates on new releases, exclusive promotions, short stories and other information, sign up for Douglas Dorow's Thriller Reader list at:

www.douglasdorow.com

Read, for the THRILL of it!

Made in the USA
Coppell, TX
31 July 2021

59769283R00152